"Tell me no, Rachel," he whispered, running a finger along her jaw. "Tell me to leave."

He ran his fingers around the back of her neck and threaded them through her hair, cupping her head in his warm palm. She watched, mesmerized, as his gaze roamed over her face. When his other hand touched her bare arm, she shivered involuntarily.

She tried to say no, tried to tell him to leave. Her lips would not form the words. But neither could she bring herself to ask him for what she feared she wanted. Her silence was the only answer she could give.

"Someday . . ." he said, trailing a finger down her arm. "Someday I want to see the same invitation in your eyes and on your lips that I see right now in this dress."

He lowered his face to hers, and for the first time in years, a man's lips touched hers.

Shock waves, warm and tingling, rushed through her. She had no defense against this tender onslaught, nor did she wish for any. . . .

WHAT ARE *LOVESWEPT* ROMANCES?

They are stories of true romance and touching emotion. We believe those two very important ingredients are constants in our highly sensual and very believable stories in the *LOVESWEPT* line. Our goal is to give you, the reader, stories of consistently high quality that may sometimes make you laugh, sometimes make you cry, but are always fresh and creative and contain many delightful surprises within their pages.

Most romance fans read an enormous number of books. Those they truly love, they keep. Others may be traded with friends and soon forgotten. We hope that each *LOVESWEPT* romance will be a treasure—a "keeper." We will always try to publish

LOVE STORIES YOU'LL NEVER FORGET
BY AUTHORS YOU'LL ALWAYS REMEMBER

The Editors

Loveswept ® 613

Janis Reams Hudson
Truth or Dare

BANTAM BOOKS
NEW YORK · TORONTO · LONDON · SYDNEY · AUCKLAND

TRUTH OR DARE

A Bantam Book / May 1993

*If you would be interested in receiving protective vinyl
covers for your Loveswept books, please write to this
address for information:*

Loveswept
Bantam Books
P.O. Box 985
Hicksville, NY 11802

ISBN 0-553-44349-6

Published simultaneously in the United States and Canada

---

*Bantam Books are published by Bantam Books, a division of
Bantam Doubleday Dell Publishing Group, Inc. Its trademark,
consisting of the words "Bantam Books" and the portrayal of
a rooster, is Registered in U.S. Patent and Trademark Office
and in other countries. Marca Registrada. Bantam Books,
1540 Broadway, New York, New York 10036.*

PRINTED IN THE UNITED STATES OF AMERICA

OPM   0 9 8 7 6 5 4 3 2 1

To Judy L., for giving me the idea.
Thanks, friend.

One

Jared Morgan tapped his pencil against his desk pad, his irritation growing along with the number of little pencil marks on the white paper. After a while he switched ends and tapped the eraser instead of the lead, cursing softly while he waited for the next applicant.

He'd been through four interviews this morning, and a more unqualified lot of applicants he'd never seen. Was he going to end the week without finding a new secretary?

Somewhere out there in the world there had to be a good executive secretary who wanted to work for a living and could type a cool hundred words a minute. A dedicated, highly intelligent, college-educated career secretary.

Jared rose reluctantly to greet his last applicant before lunch. The rush of hope he felt as the woman firmly shook his hand transformed his scowl of frustration into a smile. The smile some claimed had melted the hearts of countless women faltered somewhat as he realized it had little or no effect on the woman before him.

But that was good! Great, in fact!

She wore flat shoes, like the ones his twelve-year-old daughter wore; her skirt was too long to be attractive and hung loosely on her shapeless hips. She had no breasts to speak of, but it was hard to tell because of the way her suit jacket hung limply from her shoulders. No makeup at all, and her straight black hair, cut even with her jawline, swung forward and covered half her face. Long thick bangs nearly obscured the most hideous pair of glasses he'd ever seen. They had thick square black frames, and the lenses, not quite dark enough for sunglasses, were tinted slightly green. They cast a greenish pallor over her entire face, with a little help from the fluorescent lighting and the pea-soup color of her suit.

The word "nerd" came to mind.

And she wasn't the least impressed with his most devastating smile. His dream secretary come to life. With a twist. This one reminded him of the old-maid librarians from his childhood, those fierce, intimidating women mentally and emotionally equipped to keep small children in line with one hand and command entire armies with the other. Rachel Fredrick looked absolutely perfect. Now . . . if only she could type.

"Please have a seat, Ms. Fredrick," Jared offered.

"Thank you." The woman seated herself primly on the edge of the chair in front of his desk, laid her purse in her lap, and folded her hands and rested them precisely in the middle of her patent-leather handbag.

Patent leather. As far as he could remember, the only times he'd seen a woman with a patent-leather purse were at church on Easter Sunday and at funerals.

He flipped through the papers she handed him. The application was neat and clean, and the letters from the employment agency regarding her qualifications were impressive, to say the least. He was familiar with that particular agency, had used it before, and its management seldom, if ever, went to the trouble to write letters of recommendation. If she was half as good as her references indicated, his troubles were over.

"It says here you've just recently moved to Oklahoma City, Rachel. May I call you Rachel?" At her nod of acquiescence he continued, "What made you choose to leave St. Louis? I don't mean to pry—I'm just curious."

"That's quite all right, Mr. Morgan."

"Jared, please," he interrupted. *That voice.* How could a nerd have the sexiest voice he'd ever heard?

"Jared," she acknowledged. "I moved here to be near family."

"Then you plan to stay in the area?" He certainly didn't want to hire anyone who was just passing through. But then the firm set to her mouth told him she probably would never admit to that if she wanted this job. And she sure looked eager enough.

Out of the corner of his eye Jared noted *The Morning Movie* fading to black on one of the monitors mounted on the wall over Rachel Fredrick's left shoulder. *Time to pay the bills*, he thought as he subconsciously waited for the commercial to begin.

"Yes," she answered. "I've made Oklahoma City my home."

"Have you ever worked in a television station before?"

Jared had been general manager of Channel 3 for the past two years and was proud of his station's standing in the community. The last thing he wanted was a secretary who thought she could either become a star or meet celebrities by working in broadcasting. But this woman looked like she had entirely too much common sense to be bothered with any sort of celebrity status—her own or anyone else's.

"No, I haven't. Is that a problem, Mr. Morgan?"

"Jared."

"Jared. Is that a problem?"

"No." He glanced at the wall again and noticed the Channel 3 monitor was still black. He frowned. It had to have been longer than ten seconds by now, and ten seconds of black had better mean the master-control operator had just suffered a heart attack, as far as Jared was concerned. Two seconds, three maximum. That's all there should ever be.

"Excuse me a minute, Rachel." He reached for the phone to call and ask what the devil was going on, but then thought better of the idea. If there was a problem, which there obviously was, the last thing the engineers in the control room needed was a ringing telephone. And if they stopped in the middle of a crisis to answer the phone, he'd probably fire the lot of them.

He kept his eyes on the black screen and hesitated. They were good people in the control room. Whatever was wrong, they were undoubtedly working on it. He'd only be in the way if he went back there right now.

But there had better be a damned good reason for so much black on the air.

An instant later Jared would have loved to have seen that black again. The screen on the wall went from black to snow. Channel 3 was off the air.

"Damn." Jared jumped to his feet and ran for

the door. "Excuse me," he called back to Rachel as he left her alone in his office.

Rachel Fredrick frowned and watched him leave. His departure was accompanied by a shout from somewhere down the hall. She wondered what was going on. Surely, he wouldn't be long.

She sat still for fifteen minutes, gripping the edge of her purse until her fingers went numb. Was he ever coming back? He *had* to come back. This seemed to be the only decent-paying job available in the entire city, and she was determined to have it. She knew she was more than qualified, and if Jared Morgan had met anyone whom he really wanted to hire, he would have already hired the person and canceled Rachel's interview. That had already happened to her once.

In fact, this was the first actual interview she'd had since she started searching for a job last week. And she was determined to nail this job.

The desk before her was neat and clean in the middle, but the outer edges were piled haphazardly with papers, ledgers, and books of all sorts. The same was true of the credenza on the far wall and the sofa behind her. This man needed help. Correction—he needed *her* help.

Now, how to convince him?

As if in answer to her question, the phone on Jared Morgan's desk started buzzing, and three lights flashed. At the same time she could hear the phone in the outer office, presumably the secretary's. If she was going to answer those calls, it wouldn't seem quite so presumptuous if she at least did it from the secretary's desk.

"No, I'm sorry, ma'am, I don't know how long he'll be . . . I'll be sure to tell him." Rachel looked up from what seemed like the ninetieth phone call to see a boy leaning against the doorframe leading to the hall and grinning. She guessed his age at about nineteen. She nodded at him and returned his smile while she wrote down the caller's phone number. "Yes, ma'am," she said into the phone. "Just as soon as he returns."

"Hi," the boy at the door said when she hung up the phone. "You Rachel Fredrick?" At her nod he thrust his hands into his hip pockets. "Boss wanted me to make sure you were still here. He said to tell you he shouldn't be too much longer, if you can wait. I'm Bobby Johnson. I'm the page."

"The page?" she asked. "What does a page do?"

"Oh, you know," the boy answered with a shrug. "I take care of the mail, run around town delivering and picking up things, that sort of stuff. I guess you could say I'm the station gofer."

Rachel had learned years ago that first impressions weren't always to be trusted, but still, she liked this boy with the friendly smile. "Do you enjoy what you do?"

"It'll do for now." He shifted his weight from one foot to the other. "I studied film at a special course they had at the University of Central Oklahoma last summer. What I really want to do is be a film editor. But there haven't been any openings, so I took this job to sort of get my foot in the door."

A disembodied female voice came over the intercom: "Bobby Johnson, come to the mail room. Bobby Johnson, to the mail room, please."

Bobby straightened and took his hands from his pockets. "That's me. Gotta run. Boss said he'd like you to wait for him if you have time. See ya." With a short two-fingered wave he took off down the hall at a trot.

•   •   •

When Jared stepped from the hall into his outer office, he did a quick double take and stopped dead in his tracks. When he'd left this room forty-five minutes ago, it had looked a lot like his own office, with stacks of papers all over the desk.

Now the desk was neat and uncluttered. The paperwork had been moved to the top of the low lateral file cabinets along the back wall, the ashtrays were clean, the empty coffee cups were gone, and the overflowing wastebasket had been emptied.

He walked through the room and stepped into his own inner office. The only changes here were the clean ashtrays, the missing dirty cups, and two neat stacks of papers in the center of his desk. The rest of the piles were, thankfully, just as he'd left them.

The two new stacks were as much a puzzle as the neat appearance of his nonexistent secretary's office. One pile was a stack of pink "while-you-were-out" messages. The other appeared to be letters, typed on his own company stationery.

Someone had definitely been busy.

A tinkling of glass and the sound of running water led him to the small kitchen off the back of his office.

There stood his fantasy secretary at his sink, apparently engrossed in cleaning up the dirty glasses and week-old coffee dregs on the countertop. The woman who normally cleaned up at night had been sick for days. Jared hadn't realized what a mess the place was in, but he certainly didn't expect his secretary—much less an applicant—to do this sort of work. "What are you doing?"

At the sound of his voice Rachel's heart gave

a little flip. She nearly dropped the cup she was rinsing. "Oh! You startled me." She closed her eyes briefly to regain her composure. "I didn't hear you come in." She placed the cup in the sink and dried her hands on a dish towel. "I just thought I'd make myself useful while I waited. I hope you don't mind," she added, a bit uncertain of his reaction.

When he'd left the room earlier, his charcoal suit and burgundy tie had been neat and crisp. Now his jacket was gone, his shirt was wrinkled and dirty, and his tie hung loosely from his fingers. "I made fresh coffee. You'll pardon me if I say you look like you could use some."

Jared chuckled ruefully and ran a hand through his thick wavy hair. "I sure could."

She poured him a cup.

He took it and thanked her. "Pour yourself one and come back to the office."

Rachel declined the coffee. The shape her stomach was in, coffee was the last thing she needed. She preceded him out of the kitchen, wondering what he'd say about everything she'd done. Wondering if he'd hire her.

He leaned back in his chair with a sigh, then sipped the coffee. "Someone's been busy. What's all this?" he asked, indicating the stacks of letters and messages on his desk.

"I hope you don't think it too presumptuous of me," Rachel said, "but the phone kept ringing, and no one seemed to be around. I just took a few messages, that's all." She made a conscious effort to keep from fidgeting. What she'd actually done in his absence was take over his office, but she hoped he wouldn't see it that way.

He eyed her carefully. "And these letters?"

"I'm sorry if I overstepped, but it just looked like

an awful lot needed to be done. I didn't mind help-ing out. And please don't feel obligated to hire me because of this." She nearly choked on the words. Obligated was exactly how she wanted him to feel. Obligated enough to hire her.

"You don't want the job?"

She swallowed a knot of panic. "Of course I want the job."

He studied her a moment longer, then reached for his phone—which had miraculously stopped ringing as soon as he'd come back to the office—and punched in a three-digit number.

"Mark, this is Jared. Put a Ms. Rachel Fredrick on the payroll as of an hour ago. You can have her fill out the necessary paperwork Monday. She's going to be too busy today. Thanks."

Rachel nearly wilted with relief. "Thank you, Mr. Morgan. Jared. You won't regret it."

"I'm sure I won't, Rachel. I just hope you don't. You've got your work cut out for you."

"Oooh, Mother, what happened to your hair? Yuck."

"Caroline, is that any way for a twelve-year-old to talk to her mother?" Rachel asked with a raised eyebrow and a quirk on her lips. "Yuck, indeed. This happens to be a wig."

"But . . . why? You look so . . . so . . . like a . . ."

"I think what Caro is trying to say," Mike offered, "is that you look like a bag lady. Please tell us you didn't go on your job interview looking like that."

"I most certainly did," Rachel replied calmly as she looked up at her seventeen-year-old son. He was several inches taller than she. He had his father's height, but not his looks, thank God. She wouldn't have been able to bear it if either of her children even remotely resembled Hank. A coldness poured through her at the mere thought of her ex-husband.

"What did you do that for?" Mike demanded. "And those clothes!"

"I did it so I wouldn't look like me. And I got the job. So there."

"Well, you oughtta be able to keep this job." Caroline giggled behind her hand. "It's for sure nobody's gonna recognize you when you look like that."

"That, my darling children, is the entire idea."

"Where are you working? What kind of place is it?" Mike wanted to know.

"I'll tell you all about it, but first let me get out of this costume."

Mike and Caroline both laughed at her strange appearance as Rachel went down the hall toward her bedroom.

"Love the wig, Mom," Mike called after her.

Caroline's squeal of laughter accompanied his words. "The glasses are my favorite."

Rachel closed the door to her room and kicked off the tacky flat shoes. She rushed to rid herself of the layers of clothing as quickly as possible. How long would it take her to get used to wearing clothes so loose they threatened to fall off every time she moved?

Except for the bra. It had the opposite problem in that she'd purposely bought it two sizes too small, to flatten her chest. It wasn't all that uncomfortable after the first hour or so, but getting it off was certainly a relief.

The clothes concealed her figure, and that's what she wanted.

With the offending garments in a heap at her

feet, she reached to pull the pins from her scalp. The black wig landed like a dead thing on her dresser. She shook out her hair until it hung down her back in curls that fell halfway to her waist.

"Ah." It felt so good to be out of the disguise. But the wig and ill-fitting clothes had served her well. She had the job, and she intended to keep it. So she'd just better get used to the idea of wearing those awful clothes and that hideous wig.

When she rejoined her children, Mike said, "Now you look like the mother we know and love."

Rachel had to admit she certainly felt more like herself in her snug-fitting jeans and loose T-shirt. "The bag lady is no more . . . until Monday morning. Now tell me how your day went. How are you two making out at your new schools?"

Mike complained about being forced to read *A Tale of Two Cities*. Rachel laughed at the face he made and promised to buy him two new Louis L'Amours if he got a good grade on his book report.

"I had a great day," Caroline said. "I signed up for a girls' softball team."

"That's wonderful," Rachel said with enthusiasm. She knew Caroline had worried she might not get to play this year. "Tell us about it."

"I don't know much, really. Except that my new friend, Debbie, you remember hearing about her. Well, her dad's the coach, and she says they've already started practice, but that they need a good shortstop. And that's me! It's some sort of inner-city league, and they play nearly all summer. And you don't have to worry about how to get me to the games. If Mike can't take me, Debbie says there's always a bunch of car pools going on with the parents."

"Sounds like you're settling in at school pretty fast," Rachel observed.

"Well," Caroline said, "I miss all my old friends, but I'm making new ones."

"I'm glad, sweetie. You both know I hated to uproot you, especially in the middle of a school year, but I didn't have much choice. Now that I've got a job, things'll be fine, you'll see."

Mike laughed and shook his head. "You mean, now that the bag lady has a job."

"Watch it, kid." Rachel raised a fist in mock anger and shook it beneath her son's nose. "It's bad enough having strangers laugh out of the corners of their mouths when I walk by. I don't have to take it from you two."

"Yeah, but Mother," Caroline began, "isn't what you're doing, you know, changing your looks that way, isn't that kinda like . . . lying . . . sorta?"

Rachel sighed at her daughter's troubled look. "Yes, honey, it is lying, I suppose. And I don't like doing it. But I've tried being myself at jobs before, and it never worked out. Lying is never a good thing to do, but in this case it was my only choice if I wanted to get a job and keep it. That doesn't make it right, but that's what I've done."

"You've always told us liars get punished," Mike said gravely, a twinkle in his eye.

"Oh, don't worry. I'll be punished. Those clothes and that wig are so uncomfortable, I don't know how long I'm going to be able to stand them. And if I don't go blind from wearing those awful green glasses, it'll be a miracle."

Monday morning Rachel had Mike drop her off at work a half hour early. They had decided he would use the car during the day to get to school and to take Caroline to her softball practices, since Rachel really had no need to leave the office before five. She didn't want her new boss to see Mike just yet.

Jared Morgan had not asked about her marital status or if she had children, and she hadn't volunteered the information. She also hadn't told Mike and Caroline about that. They had enough problems of their own without being made to feel their mother was hiding their existence.

The first thing Rachel noticed when she got to her office was the audiocassette lying in the middle of her desk. The note taped to it was addressed to her. Jared would be late coming in this morning. The tape contained correspondence he'd dictated over the weekend, and could she please get as much of it taken care of this morning as possible, because when he got in, he'd have other things for her to do.

Rachel made her way through the tape, typing the correspondence into the computer, printing out the letters, making notes on her calendar, and taking phone messages.

She had just refilled her coffee cup for the third time when the phone rang—again. When she told the female caller that Jared wouldn't be in until later, the woman said, "That boy. I swear, sometimes I think he forgets he even has a mother at all."

"You're his mother?" Rachel asked politely, trying not to sound like a busybody.

"I am, for all the good it does me. Who am I speaking with?"

"I'm Rachel Fredrick, your son's new secretary."

"New secretary? Hallelujah! How long have you been working for him?"

"Actually, this is my first full day."

"And he ran off and left you there alone, did he? Well, I sympathize with you, Rachel. If he can forget he has a mother for weeks on end, I can just imagine how he treats his secretary. But you hang in there. If you're any good at your job, then he sure needs you. And if you aren't any good, he wouldn't have hired you in the first place."

"I guess you're right about that. He certainly seems to know what he's doing," Rachel said.

The two women chatted for a few more minutes. When Rachel hung up, she leaned back in her chair and smiled to herself. She'd never made a friend over the telephone before, but she had the most pleasant feeling that was what had just happened. She closed her eyes briefly and let her smile widen.

She was startled back to the here and now by Jared Morgan's deep voice from a few feet away.

"Does that smile on your face mean that call was *not* a viewer complaining about the amount of bare skin on Saturday night's late show?" He was leaning against the door to the hall, looking as crisp and neat as he had when she'd first seen him last Friday morning.

There was one other thing Rachel hadn't told her children about this new job. She hadn't told them that Jared Morgan, her new boss, was probably the best-looking man she'd ever seen. Maybe his individual features weren't exactly perfect—then again, maybe they were—but they certainly went together well.

And he had the most incredible green eyes. Jungle cats all over the world were probably jealous of those eyes, and the long, thick dark lashes that curled over them.

What in the world she was doing speculating about her boss's looks was beyond her. Flustered, both at her thoughts and at being caught relaxing when there was work to be done, Rachel straightened in her chair.

"Do you always sneak up on a person that way, Mr. Morgan?" she asked in self-defense. She regretted it immediately. That wasn't exactly the proper way to endear herself to her new boss. When he just shrugged, she continued, letting her smile return, "Actually, that wasn't a viewer on the phone. It was your mother calling to see if you were still alive."

"Damn." Jared laughed and shook his head. "That woman is always two steps ahead of me."

Rachel found herself smiling with him. "She'll forgive you for not calling if you'll at least write her a letter."

When he knew her better, Jared intended to ask Rachel Fredrick why the hell she deliberately tried to make herself look dowdy. It had to be deliberate. No one with a smile like that, and such a sexy voice, could possibly come across as a nerd without some real effort.

That subject, however, was for later. He took the papers she handed him and thumbed through them, amazed by what he saw. "You got all these done this morning?"

"Yes. I'll be able to go even faster after I've figured out the word-processing software on the computer." She patted the side of the monitor before her.

"That damned thing," Jared cursed. "What's the matter with it?"

"Nothing that I know of," she answered, one brow quirked in surprise above the rim of the hideous green glasses. "I just haven't learned what all these bells and whistles do. I've never used software with this many features before."

"If it doesn't do what it's supposed to, or if you don't like it, we'll send it back."

"Don't you dare. It's a great system."

Rachel laughed, and the sound of it sent shivers down Jared's spine. It felt smooth, like warm pudding oozing over his skin. It also relieved his ill humor, and he smiled as he strode toward his office. "Any other calls besides my mother?"

As she followed him to his desk, Rachel scolded herself. She wasn't supposed to be laughing and friendly. That only led to unpleasantness in the long run. She was supposed to be cool and efficient. A top-notch secretary.

"Yes," she replied briskly, all business now. "Todd Hargrave stopped by and said when you get time, come back to engineering and he'll detail for you what happened last Friday that put the station off the air, and Susan King from the sales department came to ask you to speak at next month's AWRT meeting."

"Did she say what I'm supposed to speak about?" Jared asked warily.

"They'd like you to speak about how more women can get into upper management in broadcasting. They want the male viewpoint. I take it AWRT is a women's group?"

"American Women in Radio and Television," Jared supplied. "Who else called?"

"Ted Parson's secretary called to remind you about the Oklahoma City Broadcasters' meeting this Thursday morning. Then Peter Michaelson in news called to let you know he's ready to start looking for a new reporter to add to his staff."

Jared nodded in acknowledgment and motioned for her to continue.

"Harve Kennedy called," Rachel said. "The corporate meeting is three weeks from tomorrow. I put a note on your calendar as a reminder. He said the rooms are all booked at the Dunes in Las Vegas, but you should make your own travel arrangements."

"Damn," Jared muttered. "They've moved it up two weeks. That means you and I will probably need to put in some late hours to get all the reports ready that I have to take with me. Will that be a problem for you, working late?"

"No," Rachel replied. *It'll make me wish I got paid by the hour, instead of by the month, but maybe you'll appreciate my efforts so much, you'll give me a raise.* "It won't be a problem."

"Good. Any other calls? I hope there are no more meetings for me to attend."

"No other calls, no more meetings that I'm aware of."

"Good." Jared pushed his chair back from his desk and stood. "I'm going down to engineering to talk to Todd. I'll be back before long. Just hold down the fort. If anything terrible happens, circle the wagons and page me on the intercom."

"In case of attack, you mean." Rachel tried to keep a straight face, but it was impossible to keep her lips from twitching.

"Don't laugh," Jared warned with a smile. "It happens sometimes." When she looked at him skeptically, he said, "Just wait until our sales manager's aunt brings her class of twenty-five third graders in for a tour of the studio." As he walked out the door, he winked at her.

Winked!

It was impossible to tell which one of them was more surprised. Jared hurried down the hall frowning. He'd definitely been alone too long. Now he was winking at nerds. And this one also happened to be his secretary!

Two

If Jared Morgan had any doubts about hiring Rachel Fredrick, they disappeared over the next three weeks as she helped him prepare for the upcoming corporate meeting in Las Vegas. She might not have known anything about broadcasting, but she understood reports and statistics, and she proved herself invaluable as she helped him assemble the required information.

She also turned out to be the most easygoing woman he'd ever been around. Long hours, delayed meals, missed meals, updating the data on the same report for the fourth time because he'd left something out—nothing seemed to faze her. Not even when he left for a few hours in the late afternoons while she had to stay and work. Being general manager, with no one for him to answer to, did have its perks.

He didn't tell her he was coaching his daughter's softball team—she might not be quite *that* understanding, knowing he was out in the sunshine, playing ball with a bunch of kids, while she was chained to the desk. But she never asked where he went when he left, only when he expected to return.

No exaggerated sighs of frustration, no sullen looks, no complaints. Just total cooperation and a lot of hard work.

Jared smiled as he opened the refrigerator in his office kitchen. It was the third week of what he referred to as Rachel's "trial by fire." They had only a few days left to finish the reports he needed, and there was still a lot of work to be done. He and Rachel had both worked until after ten the previous night—they'd been doing that a lot lately—but she had managed to go shopping and restock the refrigerator before he got to work this morning.

He sighed with pleasure as he poured himself a glass of orange juice from the new carton. No one had taken such good care of him and looked after his interests so well since his mother had when he was a kid.

When he was seated at his desk a few minutes later, Rachel entered carrying an armload of papers. She must have just come from the copy machine. He set down his juice and rushed to relieve her of the burden. "You're a secretary, Rachel, not a packhorse," he said. "You're allowed to ask for help."

"Thanks," she said as he took the stack from her trembling arms. "It didn't feel that heavy till I got halfway down the hall."

"Here." He pushed her into the chair in front of his desk. "Sit. Rest. You're going to collapse if you don't slow down a little."

"I can slow down next Monday and Tuesday while you're in Las Vegas, sitting through all those meetings."

Jared frowned at the thought of endless hours in a smoke-filled room halfway across the country. He wasn't looking forward to it. "Speaking of that, why don't you take Monday and Tuesday off? You've certainly earned it."

"I can't do that," she protested. "While we've been pulling everything out of the files to go into all these reports, nobody's been putting any of it back where it belongs. I've got tons of filing to do."

"I thought you said you'd slow down while I'm gone. What are you trying to do, run yourself into the ground?"

"No," she said with a slight smile. "Just trying to make myself indispensable."

"Well, you've done that," he said, answering her smile. "In fact, when I get back from Vegas, remind me to give you a raise."

"No problem." Her lips twitching, she reached over and pulled his desk calendar to her, then flipped the pages to next Wednesday. "Give Rachel a raise," she quoted as she wrote the note.

Jared laughed. "I put my foot in it that time, didn't I?"

"You certainly did."

Rachel went back to her desk and breathed a sigh of relief when she heard Jared place a phone call. Now she could have a few minutes to herself. The hours she'd been putting in were long—she'd scarcely seen her children—and the work was hard, but she loved every minute of it. And the pay was good, even if he was only kidding about the raise.

And working at Channel 3 was fun. The people were among the friendliest she'd ever met. Even at a quarter to five in the traffic department, when they rushed to get the next day's on-air schedule done, complete with programs, commercials, and everything else that had to account for every single second of airtime from sign on to sign off, they managed to crack jokes, despite the tension.

Most of those jokes, along with the ones coming from the other offices, were in the form of appropriately, or sometimes inappropriately, applied advertising slogans. Some of the results were hilarious.

But still, things weren't all rosy. She had one slight problem that she didn't know how to cope with. The problem's name was Jared Morgan.

Actually, the problem wasn't so much him as it was her reaction to him. She could feel herself being drawn toward him, on a personal level, and it terrified her. The last time she'd met a man she felt attracted to was when she was seventeen years old, that summer she'd met Hank.

She shuddered at the mere thought of his name. She couldn't remember the good times anymore. It was as if they'd never happened. All she could recall was the way their marriage had ended.

No. She would *not* think of that.

It had ended five years ago, and she'd survived—barely. Mike and Caroline had survived—barely.

Rachel blinked and shoved the memories away. She had put them all behind her a long time ago, and no man would ever get close enough to hurt her again.

And that's what bothered her about Jared Morgan. Every day, despite her efforts in the opposite direction, she felt herself drawn closer to him. He was warm and considerate, handsome and likable. He treated her with more respect than any man she'd ever known. He seemed to genuinely like her, in spite of her tacky appearance.

Was that why she liked him so much? Because he was the first man to be nice to her in years?

But then, if he knew who she was . . . Other men had been nice to her, for a while, until they found out. . . .

But just because he was nice to her and seemed to like her didn't explain the way her heart fluttered when he came in every morning. It didn't explain the way her breath caught in her throat when she got close enough to smell his subtle after-shave, which made her want to close her eyes and inhale deeply, knowing her knees would turn to water if she did.

All those things were purely physical, she knew, but that didn't make them any easier to deal with. Was her body so starved for a man's touch that she couldn't keep him out of her mind? If that was the case, her body and her mind were both wasting their time.

Rachel slipped off her glasses and pinched the bridge of her nose between her thumb and forefinger to still the sudden throbbing behind her eyes.

That part of her life, the physical side of love, was so far behind her that she couldn't even remember what it felt like to have a man touch her with tenderness, his desire tempered with love.

A big pair of warm hands settled on her shoulders. Rachel jumped and cried out.

"Easy there," Jared murmured, massaging the knots of tension on either side of her neck. "It's only me. I knew you were working too hard. You're stiff as a board."

And she was getting stiffer by the second. She'd been so absorbed in her thoughts that she hadn't seen or heard him come in. Now she panicked. If his thumbs moved up an inch, he'd encounter the base of her wig. Down a few inches, and he'd feel how deeply her too-tight bra cut into her flesh.

She bent her head forward to let her hair hide her face while she fumbled to get the ugly green glasses back in place. "I'm fine, really," she insisted. When she shrugged her shoulders only slightly, his hands slipped away.

Another wave of panic hit her at the sudden loss of his warm touch. "I think I'll make some more coffee." She pushed her chair back and nearly ran over his feet.

Jared stuffed his hands in his pockets and followed her to the kitchen, where he leaned against the doorframe and watched her hands shake. He cleared his throat nervously. "I'm sorry, Rachel."

Rachel's eyes widened in surprise as she turned to face him. "What for?"

"I . . . made you uncomfortable. I didn't mean to."

Rachel ducked her head in embarrassment and let her hair cover her face again. She'd overreacted and made a fool out of herself. "Forget it," she said.

By later that afternoon Rachel's self-confidence was back. She was just finishing a letter for Jared when she heard a loud commotion from the direction of the lobby. She stuck her head out the door to see what was going on and was amazed to find the lobby filled to overflowing with children. A gray-haired woman in a blue flowered dress shouted to be heard over the racket.

The receptionist cringed behind the switchboard, holding a hand over her ear and shouting into the telephone, "What? You'll have to speak up! I can't hear you!"

Rachel glanced across the little heads and spotted Jared on the other side of the lobby, in the sales department. He grinned at her, then reached for the phone on the desk next to him. A second later Rachel's phone rang.

When she answered it, his familiar deep voice laughed. "I'm not one to say I told you so, but I told you so."

Rachel laughed back and stretched the phone cord so she could see Jared, who still stood there, phone to his ear, grinning at her. "You mean we're under attack?" she asked.

"Most definitely."

"The sales manager's aunt and her third graders?"

"You got it. Circle the wagons, woman," he drawled. "I'll cut back through engineering and production, then sneak up the back hall past accounting. If I can make it past Bonzo the Clown's office before the horde gets there, I just might get back to you before sundown."

Rachel smiled and hung up the phone. *Back to you.* Not back to his desk, or back to the office, but *back to you.* Something warm and tingly spread outward from the region of her heart.

Before she even had time to analyze it, he was there, striding up the hall toward her, a teasing glint in his eyes. When he stopped and stood in front of her, only inches away, something happened to her breathing.

"I made it."

There was a huskiness in his voice. The glint in his eyes took on a new character, less teasing, more . . . something. Her knees started trembling.

This can't be happening. She couldn't let herself be attracted to him. She didn't want to be.

And surely that wasn't attraction she saw in his

eyes. It wasn't possible. Not the way she looked.

She whirled away and returned to her chair. "Yes. You made it." Her smile felt brittle.

Jared purposely refrained from following her. Instead, he went into his office and closed the door.

He was crazy. That must be the answer. He'd been working too hard and had finally lost his mind. He couldn't possibly be attracted to his own secretary. It went against everything he stood for.

Especially one who dressed like a frump and wore the world's ugliest glasses. But there was something about Rachel Fredrick. That deliciously sexy voice sent chills down his spine. Hot chills. Then there was her smile, sometimes soft, sometimes teasing, always tempting.

He liked the way she laughed, when she let herself. Hell, he liked just about everything about her, except her hair, her glasses, and her clothes. Those things didn't fit the inner woman he thought was there. If she was the type of woman he thought she was, why didn't she take at least half the pride in her appearance as she did in her work? He frowned and walked to his desk. It didn't matter. She was his secretary. Off-limits.

But on his way to his desk, he couldn't help but wonder what Rachel was like away from work.

Thursday Jared's mother called. It seemed she would be in Las Vegas the same time Jared would. The two made plans to get together. When Jared mentioned it to Rachel, she smiled. "Good. I know she misses you."

Friday morning found Rachel and Jared on their hands and knees, sorting piles of reports and packing them in boxes to be shipped to Las Vegas.

"Where does this last one go?" Jared asked. "It's next year's budget."

"No, that's last year's. It goes here." She tapped the pile next to her knee.

Jared placed the budget on the proper stack.

Rachel leaned to reach another pile and used the one next to her knee to brace herself. Her long, elegant fingers splayed across the paper. Unadorned, delicate fingers that drew Jared's attention. Were they as soft and silky as they looked?

Without thinking, he reached out and stroked the shortest one, running the tip of his index finger from her smooth, unpolished nail over her small knuckle. He traced a path from there up the back of her hand to her wristbone. Beneath his fingertip he felt tension coiled under her skin.

He lifted his gaze to hers. Her lips were moist and slightly parted. Her breath seemed as reedy as his.

Sweet heaven, man, what are you doing?

Jared jerked away from her and stared down at the papers in his other hand, wondering where they'd come from. Oh, yeah. "Uh, thanks." *Morgan, you must be out of your mind. Nerds are definitely not your type.*

But there was something about her . . .

Then another voice in the back of his mind accused, *Snob.*

The phone buzzed. Rachel jumped up like a loaded spring. A very shaky loaded spring. She was grateful for the excuse to move away from Jared. "It's Harve Kennedy." She handed Jared the phone and made certain their fingers didn't touch.

Jared stared at her, a strange look in his eyes. Then he seemed to shake himself. "He's probably calling to see if we've got everything ready for Vegas." He took the phone.

Rachel took to her heels at a near run. In the ladies' room she splashed cold water on her heated cheeks. What in the world was the matter with her? All he'd done was touch her hand, and she'd gone all hot and trembly. At the mere memory a shiver raced down her spine. It was several minutes before she felt composed enough to return to her desk.

"Rachel?" Jared called from his office.

"Coming." When she stepped through his door, he was finished with his phone call and sat with his hands folded, a peculiar look on his face. "What is it?"

"Get another seat on that Sunday afternoon flight for Vegas. Your filing is going to have to wait."

"Wh-what do you mean?"

"I mean . . . you're going with me."

For a moment Rachel panicked. *He's going to spirit me away for two days and . . . and . . .* A second later she laughed at herself when she remembered her hideous disguise. *Ha! He wouldn't be attracted to someone who looks like I do.*

Then she remembered the fire that had shot up her arm at his simple touch and thought to ask herself why he had touched her. When no answer came, she panicked again.

As it turned out, his reason for taking her with him was strictly business. It seemed that the general managers in the corporation took turns each year providing a secretary to help out at the annual meeting. The woman who was to go this year had just had a death in her family, and Jared was next on the list to provide the necessary help. *So much for ulterior motives.*

Regardless of the practical, legitimate reason Jared had given her earlier in the day for her accompanying him to Las Vegas, Rachel didn't sleep well that night. She kept remembering the way he'd touched her hand. With no more than the tip of his finger, he had stirred something in her that had lain dormant for so long she'd forgotten what it felt like. Excitement. Of the physical kind. And unwelcome, at that.

She didn't want to feel heat rush through her veins, didn't want her breath to catch, her muscles to turn weak, her heart to pound. It was foolishness, all of it. There was no room in her life for such things.

Dismissing her reaction to his touch took only slight determination. What kept her from falling asleep until nearly dawn was not understanding *why* he had touched her.

He hadn't meant anything by it, she was positive. A man like Jared Morgan was not interested in a woman who showed up for work every day looking like a mouse. Or, if her kids were to be believed, a bag lady. And that was fine with her. She didn't want him—or any other man—interested in her.

Sometime during the next day, while arranging for the next-door neighbors to look after Mike and Caroline for the weekend, Rachel managed to put Friday's incident in Jared's office, and her ridiculous reaction to it, right where it belonged—away.

But she didn't sleep any better Saturday night, for she had started remembering the old days, other trips to Las Vegas. She'd spent a lot of time there when she was younger, more famous. Would anyone recognize her? If so, they were bound to remember all the stories, all the lies.

With a whimper she despised, she rolled to her other side and punched a deeper dent in her pillow, trying to get comfortable. It didn't help. She was still wide awake the next morning when she heard Mike and Caro get up.

Exhausted from lack of sleep, Rachel dragged herself from bed. This was the day she had to pack and leave for Las Vegas. She didn't want to go. She should have told Jared she couldn't. She should have made up some good excuse. She had a bad feeling about this trip, about Las Vegas . . . the memories it held. About her stupid reaction to a man's brief touch.

She shoved the green glasses up with a forefinger and caught a glimpse of herself in her dresser mirror. She broke out laughing. What did she have to worry about? Both her worries were groundless. Absolutely no one would recognize her like this, and Jared was interested only in her secretarial skills.

Sunday afternoon Mike dropped Rachel off at Will Rogers World Airport. She checked in and met Jared at the gate several minutes ahead of schedule.

He seemed dismayed to find her dressed as if going to work, but that was too bad. She didn't intend to step out of character anywhere within ten miles of him, and certainly nowhere near Las Vegas. If he expected her to dress more casually for a Sunday afternoon plane ride, that was his problem.

The plane was on time, and the flight was

smooth and uneventful. Jared was absorbed in the latest issue of *Broadcast Management*. Rachel wanted nothing more than to sleep the entire way, but she found she was too keyed up. She spent the entire trip staring out the window.

After retrieving their luggage and the boxes of reports they'd brought with them, Jared and Rachel caught a cab for the hotel. "Have you ever been to Vegas before?" he asked as they left the airport.

"A long time ago," Rachel said tightly.

They checked in at the Dunes. When she realized Jared's room was right next door to hers, Rachel felt a twinge of unease. She dismissed the feeling with a shrug. She was secure in her disguise—she had nothing to worry about.

"If you can wait a while before dinner, I'd like to see how many of the others are already here," Jared said at her door after tipping the bellman.

Rachel gave her standard answer: "No problem."

"Meet you back up here in about an hour?"

"Fine."

Jared nodded and headed for the elevator.

Rachel closed the door behind him and sagged with exhaustion. An hour. She had an hour. She kicked off her shoes, then took off her jacket and pulled out her shirttail. After unfastening the confining too-small bra, she collapsed on the bed. She was still too keyed up to sleep, but maybe lying down for a while would relax her. The detested green glasses clattered as she tossed them onto the bedside table.

She was asleep in seconds.

An hour later Jared knocked on Rachel's hall door and got no answer. Maybe she had the television on and couldn't hear him. He knocked louder. "Rachel?"

Inside the room Rachel groaned in protest at the noise intruding on her sleep. "Go away," she murmured.

The pounding came again, louder this time.

"Go . . . away."

"Rachel?"

Rachel blinked. Was that Jared's voice? Oh, heavens, she'd fallen asleep. Still groggy, she staggered toward the door.

"Rachel? Are you all right?"

"I'm coming," she mumbled. She felt rumpled beyond belief, but right then stilling that infernal pounding at her door seemed more important than straightening her clothes.

Jared pounded on the door again, worry tensing his shoulders. She had looked incredibly tired on the plane. Maybe she wasn't feeling well.

Then he heard her fumbling with the lock, and the door swung open. She hung on to the doorknob and swayed slightly. Her clothes were a mess, to say nothing of her hair. He felt like a jerk. He'd obviously awakened her.

"Sorry," he said, his gaze skimming her from head to toe again.

Something about her hair snagged his attention. Aside from being mussed from sleep, it looked . . . crooked. It came around too far on one side of her face. On the other side it started farther back than it should. It was—*I'll be damned.* It was a wig. With it pushed askew as it was, he could plainly see golden-blond hair pulled tight beneath it. Blond!

One piece of the puzzle that was Rachel Fredrick clicked into place. No wonder her skin looked so sallow and her hair didn't seem to suit her.

Her soft golden complexion was never meant to be framed in black.

It was also never meant to be shaded with green glasses. Now that she was without them, he had his first clear view of her face and eyes. He blinked. "They're blue," he said softly.

She swallowed, her face going pale. "What's blue?"

"Your eyes. They're the most incredible shade of blue."

The panic that raced across those eyes was unmistakable. Then she squinted. "Jared? I . . . I can't see. Is that you? Let me get my glasses."

Jared stuffed his hands in his pockets and bit the inside of his lip as she turned away and stumbled toward the bed. He'd bet his station's standings in the next ratings that she could see just fine without those damn green glasses.

Her hands shook as she grabbed the glasses from the nightstand beside the bed.

"You don't need them, do you?" he asked quietly.

She whipped her head around toward him. And she saw him plainly. He read that much in those startled eyes.

"Of course I do," she claimed, her voice thin and breathy. She nearly poked herself in the eye with an earpiece while trying to get the glasses on.

A dozen questions battered him. Why would she disguise herself? Why would she deliberately make herself look so unattractive?

If he were feeling reasonable, he would admit it wasn't really any of his business. If Rachel Fredrick chose to wear an ugly wig and tinted glasses that made her look washed out, that was her privilege.

Still, he couldn't seem to stop himself from

walking toward her and reaching for the glasses. "May I?"

She jerked away so fast, the glasses flew from her nose and landed on the floor next to Jared's foot. As he bent to retrieve them, she stumbled back and made a strangled sound in her throat that sounded like fear.

Jared picked up the glasses and straightened, holding them up to the light. He'd been right—they were plain tinted glass.

"Rachel?"

She flinched at the sound of his voice. The fear he thought he had imagined was plainly visible in her wide blue eyes. But it was more than fear, and it was directed at him. She was terrified—of *him.*

He wasn't sure what kind of reaction he'd expected, but her fear surprised him. Hurt him.

For one brief instant he wondered if she could be some sort of corporate spy sent by a competitor. That might explain the fear he saw.

Then he dismissed the idea. If he worked in New York or Los Angeles, or one of the other large television markets, something like that might be possible. But not in Oklahoma City. He knew his competitors, and they knew him. They might try to hire each other's employees away, but none of the men he knew would stoop to planting a spy. No way. Information was too easy to get without that. There must be some other explanation for her disguise. And her fear. "What's this all about, Rachel?"

Her response was to take another step back. Her eyes grew bigger.

"Why would you be afraid of me? Dammit, you know I wouldn't hurt you."

Rachel slumped. Of course he wouldn't hurt her. Not physically. She knew that. This was

Jared. But he could hurt her, destroy her in ways other than physical. If he found out . . .

And he would find out about her past. If he didn't recognize her yet, he soon would, surely. The minute he saw what she really looked like, without the wig, the glasses, the ill-fitting clothes.

The guilt she had fought since the day he hired her rose to her throat and choked her. Caroline's words rushed back. *Isn't what you're doing . . . lying . . . sorta?*

Rachel felt sick. Had she really hoped to get away with her deception indefinitely? Surely, she hadn't been that stupid.

But yes, she had been that stupid. That desperate.

The game, however, was up. Jared had been good to her. She *liked* him. She owed him at least part of the truth. He would probably realize the rest on his own.

With trembling hands she pulled the pins from the wig and tugged it from her head. Her hair, matted and tangled from being stuffed beneath the wig, fell down her back.

She could do that much. She could take off her wig. But she somehow couldn't force herself to look him in the face.

His voice, when he spoke, sounded . . . hurt. Confused. "Why, Rachel? Why?"

She raised her gaze to meet his but couldn't answer.

He reached up and pulled a thick strand of her hair over her shoulder. "Why would you want to hide this?" With each word his voice grew stronger, more demanding. "Why the glasses? Why the clothes that obviously don't fit? Why, Rachel?"

Rachel's heart hammered against her ribs.

Could it be true? Could he honestly not know who she was? She watched his gaze drift over her face, her hair. No flash of insight lit his eyes. It must be true. He didn't recognize her. *Thank you, God.*

"Are you going to answer me?" he asked quietly.

She dropped her gaze. "Are you going to fire me?"

Jared was startled by her question. Fire her? He hadn't thought of it. "I . . . I don't know what I'm going to do."

She had deceived him, made him feel like a fool. But what, really, had she done? She had worn a wig and a pair of glasses, and her clothes didn't particularly suit his taste.

Then he wondered . . . "Is your name really Rachel Fredrick?"

Now it was her turn to look startled. "Of course. I wouldn't lie."

"Wouldn't lie?" he cried. "Your whole appearance is a lie. Why should I believe anything else about you?"

She dropped her gaze quickly, as though his words hurt. "So you're going to fire me?"

Jared rubbed the back of his neck in frustration. "I don't know what I'm going to do," he repeated.

He watched, fascinated, as a look of determination crossed her face. She looked him in the eye and straightened her shoulders. "I'm good at my job. You've said so yourself."

"Yes, and I meant it."

"Then what difference does it make what I look like?"

"What difference? Are you crazy? Rachel, you're beautiful. Why would you want to look like . . . like this? Why the charade?"

"What difference does it make, if you're going to fire me anyway?"

"Give me a good enough reason, and maybe I won't," he offered. He saw a tiny spark of hope flare in her eyes. She must want to keep this job.

And she did want it. If she lost it, the employment agency would want to know why. If they found out what she'd done, she might not be able to get another job for quite a while, and she couldn't afford to be without one.

Aside from finances, she needed her position as Jared's secretary for other reasons. Her hectic, famous days, and the infamous ones that followed, had left her feeling adrift. She needed a straightforward, organizational sort of job, one she could exert at least a minimum of control over. She needed it to keep her feet on the ground, her head on straight, so she could rebuild her life, her own sense of self-worth.

She had started to feel those things happening since she'd gone to work for Jared. She did not want to lose the ground she'd gained. *Please, don't let me lose this job.*

She took a deep breath and decided to tell him—not the truth, not all of it, anyway. "My, uh, *looks* . . . have caused me problems on past jobs." There. That was the literal truth. Sort of.

"What?"

His bark of laughter angered her. "It's true."

Jared cocked his head sideways as he sat on the bed and looked up at her. "Are you trying to tell me that somewhere underneath all this"—he waved his hand at her clothes—"lies a body that, uh, drives men wild?"

No, that wasn't what she meant, but if that's

how he interpreted her words, so much the better. "A minute ago you said I was beautiful."

"That doesn't mean I'm on the verge of attacking you, dammit."

"You asked me why, and I told you. I can't help it if you don't believe me," she snapped. Lord, she couldn't believe she was snapping at him. *Take it easy, Rachel. Easy.* Her future rested in his hands. She couldn't afford to antagonize him.

His eyes narrowed. "So without ever having met me, without knowing anything about me, you came to my office that first day dressed like this, assuming that if you didn't disguise your . . . charms, I wouldn't be able to control myself?"

He was twisting her words, but to be fair, she supposed it was her own fault. Still, the only way she could think of to correct him would be by telling the truth, which she was not prepared to do. Cowardly or not, she intended to cling to her anonymity with both hands for as long as she could.

"No comment, huh?" His jaw tensed. "In that case, I have to tell you, I resent the hell out of your implied accusation."

"I'm not accusing you of anything," she protested.

"Then you don't believe I'm a lecher who can't control his animal instincts?"

"Of course not."

"Prove it," he challenged, a sudden gleam in his eye.

Rachel took a step back and clutched the neck of her blouse. "I beg your pardon?"

"Well, don't look at me like I expect you to strip," he said with disgust. "Just put on some clothes that fit, something dressy, and have dinner with me."

"I don't have any clothes like that with me," she said, her back stiffening at the challenge in his eyes.

"Get some."

"How?"

"The first floor of this hotel is full of shops with long, slinky evening dresses. Buy one."

"Are you kidding? You don't pay me that much. I can't afford those kinds of stores. And we're not talking about just a dress, you know. I'd have to have shoes, and if you want it done right, I'd need jewelry, a handbag, a—"

"Get them." Jared reached into his wallet and pulled out a credit card and tossed it to her.

She caught the card in midair. "You're crazy."

Yes, he thought maybe he was. What he was suggesting was inappropriate at best, and certainly outrageous. Still, he couldn't resist the dare.

"All I'm asking," he said, keeping his voice even, "is for you to trust me enough to show me the real you, and let me prove I can treat you with respect no matter what you look like. I think you owe me that much."

Rachel stalled. "I can't sign your name on a charge ticket. They'd have me arrested."

"Then I'll just have to go with you, won't I?" He stood up and motioned toward the door.

Rachel stunned herself by suddenly wanting to do as he asked, no matter how crazy it sounded. She wanted to do it for him. After deceiving him as she'd done, maybe she owed it to him. But not until she knew . . . "Are you going to fire me?" she asked again.

He stared at her long enough to make her knees quiver. Then one corner of his mouth curved up. "Not if you swear you're not an ax murderer."

Rachel felt her stomach clench. She forced a smile as best she could. "Of course I'm not."

He stared at her so long, she feared he could see clear into her soul and read all her secrets.

"Then you still have a job," he said.

Rachel stood before the mirror in her hotel room and stared at her reflection. Why was she doing this? Sure, it felt wonderful to dress in beautiful clothes again, to let her hair down and be herself for a change. But then, the image in the mirror wasn't really her. Not anymore. It looked like the old Rachel, the famous Rachel.

And that made her wonder just what she had gotten herself into. But it was too late to back down now. She had promised herself and Jared she would go through with this.

Of course, that was before she'd tried on the dress he'd chosen. The store he had selected was an expensive one, the dresses in her size sexier, more revealing, than she would have preferred.

But as she had already acknowledged, it was too late now.

She was ready fifteen minutes early and used the extra time for another coat of nail polish, as well as to bolster her resolve, which was slowly being eaten away by trepidation.

What in the world was she doing, dressing like this for a man she barely knew? And in this town, of all places—this very hotel—where she had been so well known.

"That was years ago," she told herself. Surely no one would still be around who would recognize her.

Don't count on it, a nasty little voice growled.

Well, it was too late now. She was committed. *I*

should *be committed,* she thought. *To a nuthouse.* She grimaced at her reflection in the mirror.

Revealing herself as she was, in a hotel where she would surely be recognized, was foolish. Once Jared realized who she was, would her life at Channel 3 become intolerable, as it had at her previous three jobs back in St. Louis? Would she be forced to flee the speculation, the cutting remarks, the outright ostracism of her coworkers, as she had in the past?

She squeezed her eyes shut. *Please, please, don't let Jared learn who I am.* As long as he didn't know her background, maybe she'd be safe.

Until he recognized her. Until someone else recognized her and said something to jar his memory. Surely a man involved in broadcasting would remember all those sensational news stories from a few years ago. Those stories that never seemed to die. Those stories that wouldn't let her hide, or rest, or even keep a job so she could support her children.

"Enough," she told herself.

She wiped her palms on the hand towel from the bathroom. After a few deep breaths she gave herself a final check in the mirror.

The sharp knock on her door made her flinch.

Three

At the first click of the lock Jared stopped pacing the hall and took a step toward her door. As it swung open, he got his first glimpse of the real Rachel Fredrick.

She was a golden girl, from the top of her golden curls hanging halfway to her waist to the tips of the gold high-heeled slippers on her small feet. And the dress . . . His collar suddenly felt like it was choking him.

He'd chosen the dress because it was the least revealing of any the shop had in Rachel's size. He hadn't realized . . .

It had a high turtleneck and no sleeves. The only bare skin showing was that of Rachel's face and arms. Yet it was the most provocative evening gown he'd ever seen. His mouth dried out, and he forgot to breathe.

Shimmering gold clung to her body like a second skin over her generous breasts, her rib cage, her narrow waist that he knew he could span with his hands, and it curved tightly over gently flaring hips. From there it hung straight to the floor, hiding the shape of her legs.

Sweet heaven.

She was stunning. The most stunning woman he'd ever seen in his life. This was the woman he'd been spending twelve hours a day with for the past three weeks? This golden girl?

Deep red garnets dangled from her ears. The slight blush on her cheeks, the dark wine of her lips, and the scarlet polish on her fingernails were the only other colors on her—except gold.

He stared at her for what seemed an eternity before he finally found his voice. "You are beautiful." His eyes drifted over her soft curves.

Rachel's trepidation flourished under his heated gaze. What in the world had she been thinking of to go along with his scheme? She had made a serious mistake.

She felt branded by the fire in his deep green eyes. When he just stood there staring at her, it was as if he could see right through the clinging fabric, and she was horrified to feel her nipples hardening. Would he notice?

His eyes smoldered.

He noticed! In a panic Rachel spun back into her room. His sharp intake of breath told her he'd just discovered the back of her dress. Or rather, the back of her, since the dress had no back until three inches below her waist.

She picked up the small clutch, made of the same material as the dress, and peered at him over her shoulder. "I'm ready when you are."

She sounded cool and confident—all business— until Jared looked into her eyes. The uncertainty there contrasted sharply with the warmth of her appearance, the graceful, confident set of her shoulders, the heat she generated in his blood. He blinked and looked closely at her face for the first time. She was stunning, and he felt like a fool.

How could he not have seen the perfection of her features before? No wig or pair of glasses could have hidden her loveliness.

Right now he wished like hell he'd looked at the back of that dress before he'd selected it. It wasn't covering nearly enough of her skin for his peace of mind. She probably thought he'd chosen it on purpose.

He cleared his throat nervously. "Uh, right. Dinner."

A few minutes later Rachel again admitted this entire plan was a mistake. As badly as she did not want to be recognized, she also did not want to be alone with Jared in the close, intimate confines of the elevator. But Fate, it seemed, was out to get her. How else could she and Jared have ended up alone together in the elevator at eight o'clock in a crowded Las Vegas casino hotel?

The door slid closed, sealing them in privacy. Funny, but Rachel had never suffered from claustrophobia before. She'd also never been so ill at ease with Jared before. But then, she'd never really noticed how wide his shoulders were. She tried desperately not to notice now.

If she wanted him to treat her like his secretary, she needed to act like his secretary. She cleared her throat. The sound seemed to echo in the elevator. "You never did tell me, did you find the others who came for the meeting?"

Jared saw through her attempt at normalcy but had to give her credit for trying. She was nervous as hell but was determined to ignore the fact. And she seemed to be doing a better job of it than he was.

Not that he was nervous, but maybe he should be. What had possessed him to concoct such a stupid plan as this? He was supposed to prove to her he was a gentleman, that he respected her, that he wasn't some slavering animal who intended to pounce on her any minute.

Noble sentiments, coming from a man who was having extreme difficulty keeping his response to her from becoming obvious to anyone who cared to look. With a nonchalance he was far from feeling, he slipped his hands into his trouser pockets and studied the dial above the door.

"Yeah," he told her, "I found them. You'll meet them all tomorrow."

She flipped open her purse, then closed it. "Do you think you'll get your movie plan approved?"

So help him, if she licked her lips one more time . . .

This time it was he who had to clear his throat. "We'll just have to see."

When the elevator slid to a stop, the doors opened with a soft *whoosh*. Rachel swallowed with relief.

He motioned for her to precede him out of the elevator. As she complied, she felt his eyes all over her back.

Jared folded his fingers against his palms to keep from touching her. The teasing glimpses of her bare back when her hair swayed had his chest tightening.

Rachel kept her gaze trained straight ahead as Jared led her to the door of the restaurant. The maître d' glanced at them briefly, then away . . . then back again, as though startled. A wide smile of pure delight spread across his face. His eyes held a definite twinkle as he held out his arms.

"I don't believe it," he cried. "After all this time. And you're still just as lovely as ever, Miss Rachel Anne. Welcome. Welcome back."

"Charles," Rachel cried softly.

She had assumed, or hoped, that after all these years, no one would remember or recognize her. Surely, all those people she knew in that old life were long gone from here. But if she had to be mistaken, if she had to see someone from her past, she was glad it was Charles. He'd always been more than kind to her back then.

"I never thought you'd still be here, Charles. After all this time I would have thought you'd've given up on this place and bought that little cabin up in the mountains you used to talk about," she told him, smiling brilliantly.

"What?" he exclaimed, squeezing her hands. "And miss the chance to see you again? I could never risk that, Miss Rachel Anne."

"I'll bet you say that to all the girls, Charles," she said with a smile.

"I most certainly do." The elderly, elegant gentleman sobered quickly and reestablished his dignified mien. It wouldn't do for the maître d' of one of the most elegant restaurants in Las Vegas to be seen grinning like an idiot. But his eyes twinkled merrily when he asked, "Have you come to dine with us tonight?"

"Yes, we have." She chanced a quick glance at Jared and saw a thousand questions flitting across his eyes.

"We have reservations," Jared said. "For Morgan."

"Certainly, Mr. Morgan." Charles led them to an intimate table for two on the far side of the dining room.

Nothing much had changed over the years, Rachel noted. Crisp white linen draped each table. Place settings were elegant with their fine china, crystal, and silver. Romantic, Old World charm filled the air, enhanced by white columns and strolling violinists. Too bad she didn't feel romantic. With a man like Jared Morgan at her side, a woman should feel warm and excited, not cold and nervous. The atmosphere was wasted on her.

As soon as she and Jared were seated, a waiter rushed over and tugged on Charles's sleeve. "That's the table you had me set up for Mr. Newton. He doesn't have a show tonight, and he'll be here in ten minutes," the man said frantically.

Instead of answering, Charles stepped aside and waved his hand toward Rachel with a flourish. The waiter's eyes widened with surprised delight. His lips formed a soundless "Oh" before he recovered himself and bowed at the waist. "Good evening, sir," he said to Jared. Then: "Miss Rachel Anne . . . may I get you a glass of Chablis?"

Jared's eyebrows rose, while Rachel smiled graciously. "You remembered. How kind. Thank you, Thomas, I'd love it."

Thomas beamed, took Jared's drink order, then turned aside to Charles. "I'll put Mr. Newton over next to the kitchen door."

Jared folded his arms across his chest and eyed her carefully. "I'm intrigued," he said. "Just how is it that a secretary from St. Louis can travel halfway across the country and get treated like royalty in one of the most exclusive restaurants around?"

Rachel shrugged and lowered her gaze from his penetrating stare. "I've been here before, that's all."

"So I gathered."

Just then Thomas brought their drinks, and Rachel had to force herself to keep from hiding behind her wineglass. This was not going the way she'd hoped. Not at all. She didn't know what she had hoped for—maybe a giant hole to open in the floor and swallow her up. She had prayed for enough strength and calm to make it through dinner, yet both seemed to fade with each look from Jared's deep green eyes.

"So your name really is Rachel," he said.

She took a deep breath, then a sip of wine. "I told you it was."

"And that's about all you've told me," he said. "I'm waiting for some answers, Rachel."

"I haven't heard the questions yet."

Before he could start in on her, his attention was caught and held by a stately dark-haired woman of around sixty who approached their table. Jared's eyes widened in surprise, and he rose swiftly to his feet. "Mother. I didn't expect to see you until tomorrow."

Cynthia Morgan turned her cheek for the expected kiss. Her gaze lingered on Rachel for a moment before looking back at her son. "Same here, dear," she said. She waved toward a table for six near the front entrance. "We were having dinner when I saw you come in. Are you going to introduce us?" she asked, smiling toward Rachel.

"Of course. This is Rachel Fredrick, my secretary. Rachel, my mother, Cynthia Morgan. I believe the two of you have met over the phone."

"We certainly have," Mrs. Morgan said with a smile. "So you're Rachel."

"How do you do?" Rachel said. "It's nice to finally meet you in person after talking with you over the phone."

"Yes." Mrs. Morgan eyed her steadily, a puzzled look on her brow. Then suddenly her eyes cleared. "Of course! Rachel Anne! I don't know why I didn't recognize you sooner. Well, this is wonderful! Jared, why on earth didn't you tell me?"

Rachel felt her throat close with fear.

"Tell you?" Jared said. "I wish someone would tell me."

"You mean you don't know? . . ." Her words were cut off by the sudden look of panic and pleading in Rachel's eyes.

Please, Rachel thought. *Please don't tell him.*

Cynthia chose her words carefully. "Of course you wouldn't have known," she said. "Rachel Anne used to be a famous model, years ago. It was back when you were down in Puerto Rico putting that new television station on the air. You and Debbie were down there longer than I thought, if you can't recognize one of the most famous faces in the country."

Rachel held her breath, waiting for Jared's mother to tell the rest. After a moment Rachel blinked, then swallowed with relief when she realized Mrs. Morgan wasn't going to say anything else—for now. She gave a silent thank-you for the woman's discretion, for she was certain Cynthia Morgan knew every detail of the rest of Rachel's secrets.

Some secrets! Everybody over the age of ten in the entire country knew all about Rachel Anne and what had happened several years ago. Everyone except, thank God, Jared Morgan. There was no recognition of her past on his face at all.

Jared and his mother spoke for a few more minutes, promising to meet the next day for lunch. Rachel used the time to collect herself and gather her wits. No damage had been done, she decided. If she played her cards right and was careful, Jared might just think her career in modeling was all she'd been hiding.

"So," he said after his mother had returned to her table of friends.

Rachel pleated her napkin against her lap.

"A model, huh?"

Her stomach knotted. "Yes."

Silence stretched uneasily between them, broken only by the tinkling of fine crystal and silver and the violinists, who paused at their table for a moment, then moved on.

Jared and Rachel placed their orders with Thomas. When the meal arrived, Rachel picked at the crabmeat on her plate, her appetite squelched under Jared's steady, heated regard.

His gaze locked on her face. "I thought most models were just empty-headed decoration."

"I believe you just answered your own question," Rachel said, sticking with the half-truth she'd given him earlier in the day.

It took him only a moment to follow what she meant. "You think if I'd known you'd been a model, I wouldn't have taken you seriously when you applied for the job."

"Can you deny it?"

His brows came together over the bridge of his nose. "Yes, I can and do deny it."

"Even after that statement you just made?"

He pursed his lips and gave her a wry grin. "Touché. I guess I'm not quite as fair-minded as I thought."

"Most people aren't," Rachel muttered.

They fell silent for a few minutes, until Jared asked, "How did you get to be such a good secretary?"

"So you admit I'm a good secretary?"

"That was never in question. I'd just like to know how it happened. Why did you change careers? Judging by the reaction you've received here, I'm surprised you'd give up that kind of fame and fortune."

Rachel lowered her gaze and swirled her fork around in her food. "It did pay well. But that kind of life, always in the public eye, can be pretty crazy. I got tired of living in the middle of a three-ring circus. I needed a little sanity. A slower pace. Something more stable."

"But why a secretary? Most women I know think being a man's secretary is . . . demeaning, or something. I thought all women wanted to be the boss these days."

"Not all women." Rachel shook her head slightly. Her gaze swept up to his, then down again as she sipped her wine. "I've never thought of it as demeaning. It's what I'd always wanted to be, before I took up modeling. I like to work with details. I like to type. I like to organize things. When I retired from modeling, I went back to school and took the courses I needed to get me started."

She gave a sad little chuckle. "No executive can survive without a secretary or assistant. I used to think that if I was good enough at my job, I'd have some security. As long as I did my work, and did it well, I'd be needed. I've learned the hard way, that's not always true."

Jared started to speak, then stopped as the waiter appeared to clear away their plates and offer dessert. Jared and Rachel both declined the sweets.

Jared studied her a moment longer, then signaled for the check.

On the way to the elevator, without thinking, he placed his hand on the bare skin of her lower back. But even when she flinched at his touch, he couldn't bring himself to take his hand away. He kept it there against her silken flesh and guided her through the throngs of people.

Each slight movement of his fingers seemed to make Rachel shiver. By the time they reached her room a few minutes later, she was shaking so hard, he had to take the key from her icy fingers and open the door for her.

What now? Rachel's frantic mind cried. Somewhere along the way, her nerve had disappeared completely and left her defenseless. Whatever happened now would be entirely her fault. He didn't know about her past, but that seemed to be the least of her worries. She'd teased him by wearing this damn dress, and he had responded. The heat was plain in his eyes, in the feel of his hand against her back.

She stepped away from that hand and turned to face him.

"May I come in?" he asked from the doorway.

Rachel shivered. "Why?"

"We need to talk."

"No, we don't."

"Okay," he said, "*I* need to talk."

Tell him no. Send him away! her mind screamed. But his eyes, while still lit with heat, also held a sincerity she couldn't deny. "All right," she whispered. "Come in."

He followed her into the room and pushed the door closed behind him. The loud click of the latch echoed ominously in her ears. She flinched at the sound. Turning her back on him, she dropped her clutch on the dresser, folded her arms protectively across her abdomen, and stared out the sliding glass doors at the bright lights below.

"What did you want to talk about?" She was surprised at the steadiness of her voice when her whole body was trembling.

"I owe you an apology, and a compliment," he said.

She turned toward him in surprise.

"It must have taken a great deal of courage for you to go along with my ridiculous plans for tonight. Judging by my own prejudicial remark about models, and some of the stares you were getting from more than a few men, I can't say I blame you for anything you've done."

Oh, if only he knew *all* she'd done. He would take those words back so fast . . .

"I learned a little something about myself tonight too." He pushed his jacket aside and slipped his hands into his pants pockets. "Something I'm not sure how to deal with."

He looked troubled, and Rachel had the sudden urge to offer comfort. She smothered it quickly.

"I think I'm a fraud."

Rachel blinked. "What?"

He gave a harsh laugh and studied the ceiling a moment. "I wanted you to put on that sexy dress and spend the evening with me so I could prove what an upstanding gentleman I am. I like to think of myself as a gentleman. I wanted to show you that to me you are first, above anything else, a person I like spending time with, whom I enjoy working with."

His words eased some of the tightness in her chest. He had no idea how soothing they were to her, how much she desperately needed to hear them.

"You're the best secretary I've ever had, and I don't want anything to interfere with our working relationship, or with whatever friendship we might have."

"Thank you," she whispered. "But how does that make you a fraud?"

"I guess the least I can do is be an honest fraud," he said. "I meant everything I just said to you. But despite all that, I still want very much to kiss you."

Rachel sucked in a sharp breath of denial. If she were to be as honest as Jared, she had to admit her silent denial was not in response to his words, but to the hot tingling rushing through her veins at the thought of being kissed by him.

Her body's reaction was impossible to deny. It might have been years since a man had stirred her senses, but she knew desire when she felt it. His words left her shaken. She didn't want to feel, didn't want to want.

In her past she had managed to generate only two different responses from men, lust or dismissal. If she gave in to the yearnings she felt, what would Jared be—an attacker, or a disappointed lover? She didn't want to know . . . couldn't take the risk of finding out.

He came closer, until he stood directly before her. She could feel the heat from his body through her gown. There was nowhere to go. One step back and she'd be against the balcony door. One step forward was Jared's chest.

"Tell me no, Rachel," he whispered, running a finger along her jaw. "Tell me to leave."

Her heart thundered in her chest. She told herself it thundered in fear.

He ran his fingers around the back of her neck and threaded them through her hair, cupping her head in his warm palm. She watched, mesmerized, as his gaze roamed over her face. When his other hand touched her bare arm, she shivered involuntarily.

She tried to say no, tried to tell him to leave. Her lips would not form the words. But neither could she bring herself to ask him for what she feared she wanted. Her silence was the only answer she could give.

"Someday . . ." he said, trailing a finger down her arm. "Someday I want to see the same invitation in your eyes and on your lips that I see right now in this dress."

He lowered his face to hers, and for the first time in over five years, a man's lips touched hers. His lips were soft, warm, gentle. The kiss was tentative and undemanding and exhilarating.

Shock waves, warm and tingling, rushed through her. She had no defense against this tender onslaught, nor did she wish for any. She stood paralyzed, unable to move, not responding except for the rapid increase in her pulse and breathing.

Jared pulled back and looked at her. In her eyes he saw the same startled wonder that he was feeling. Something was happening here—something important—and he wanted to explore it more thoroughly. The pulse pounding along her temples matched the rapid thundering of his heart. His hands trailed down her silken arms until he reached her fingers. He grasped her hands and brought them to his shoulders, where he held them until he was assured by the movement of her fingers that they would stay.

Rachel felt his large, warm hands settle on the curve of her waist. And then he kissed her again. But this kiss was different. She felt his barely controlled passion, and as his lips took hers, she felt their plea. They reached for her, yearned for her, begged her to open herself to their demand. They seemed to say, *This move was mine. The rest is up to you.*

Emotions long dormant shimmied to life as his kiss became more insistent, and the sensuous woman buried deep inside her for so many years responded. Her fingers dug into the smooth fabric of his dinner jacket. Her mouth opened to his.

His tongue immediately darted within to explore, to taste, to tease, and soon her own tongue joined in the dance. When she ran it along the sleek, silky underside of his, she felt a deep groan come from his throat. His arms circled around and pulled her tightly against his chest.

It was impossible to tell whose heart was pounding harder until Jared slipped a hand around and settled it possessively over her breast. He turned her a little, for better access, and Rachel could only cling to him as his hard palm closed over her full, firm flesh, nothing separating their skin but the thin layer of gold lamé.

She trembled with the force of feelings she'd never thought to feel again, feelings she wasn't sure she'd ever felt before. His thumb flicked over her nipple, and it instantly hardened. Liquid warmth pooled deep inside her. This time it was Rachel who groaned.

Her response intoxicated him. He felt her hands slide around his neck until they clutched frantically at the back of his head, holding him there where he most wanted to be. He pressed his hips against her and knew she could feel the evidence of his arousal against her stomach.

At the first touch of his hardness against her abdomen, Rachel panicked. The here and now receded, and the past swept forward, smothering her in gaping darkness and icy fear. Rationally, she knew it was Jared who held her. Jared wouldn't hurt her. But sheer terror left no room for rational thoughts. The panic overwhelmed her, and she fought for her life, squirming, shoving, trying to break free of the arms that imprisoned her.

Jared felt the change in her instantly but didn't understand she was trying to get free until she tore her mouth from his and he saw her eyes. God, her eyes. He'd never seen such terror in his life.

"Rachel?"

With an anguished cry she broke loose of his arms and stumbled backward against the balcony door.

Rachel cried out again as her head struck the glass door. Blood rushed in her ears until all she could hear was a loud roar. Panting, she had but one thought: escape.

Four

She had to escape the huge, menacing body bending toward her. Escape the large hand that reached for her. "No!" She pushed back against the door and held out her hands to ward him off. "No!"

He backed off. Thank God, he backed off. His lips moved, but she heard nothing over the roar of her own blood, the rasp of her own breath.

It seemed as though she huddled there against the door forever, shaking, shaking so hard. Freezing. She was so cold.

"Rachel?"

The voice penetrated this time. She blinked to clear her vision, shocked to feel moisture trickling down her cheeks. "Jared?"

"It's me. You're safe. Do you hear me?" His voice lured her out of the darkness and terror. "You're safe, Rachel."

Slowly, slowly, Jared saw sanity creep back into her eyes. Nothing in his life had shaken him the way her terror just had. His heart pounded. He ached with the need to comfort her, yet he didn't dare touch her.

"Rachel? Are you all right?" *Stupid question, Morgan.*

But she gave him a shaky nod. "I"—she paused to suck in a deep lungful of air—"I'm . . . sorry." Then her knees buckled.

Reflex had him reaching to catch her before he could stop himself. He held his breath, praying his sudden touch wouldn't set her off again.

She fell against him, then tried to straighten. "I'm okay."

The hell you are. "I know. It's all right. Here." He led her toward the armchair in the corner. "Sit down a minute and catch your breath."

He eased her onto the chair and reluctantly let her slip from his arms. Kneeling before her, he pushed her hair back from her face. "Better?"

Nodding, Rachel sniffed and closed her eyes. Oh, God, how would she ever face him again? She couldn't believe what had just happened to her.

She felt Jared move away, but she refused to open her eyes. A moment later he was back.

"Here, have a sip."

She opened her eyes and stared at the glass of water he held out. When she reached for it, her hand shook so violently, he had to help her get the glass to her lips. After she took a sip, he set the glass on the floor beside her chair. "Thank you," she managed.

"You're welcome."

She wanted to cry at the way he carefully modulated his voice, as if afraid one wrong word, even a wrong tone, would send her into another fit of panic.

"Do you want to talk about it?" he asked softly.

Talk about it? She couldn't even bear to think about it. "I'm sorry."

"Would you quit saying that? It's my fault. I shouldn't have rushed you. I should have—"

"No," she cried. "It's not your fault. I just panicked, all right? I'm sorry. I . . . I had a bad experience once. It was a long time ago. I . . . I thought I was over it."

She hadn't meant to say so much. As she saw a taut stillness come over him, she wanted to call back the words.

Jared felt ice creep through his veins. "Were you raped?"

She shook her head and swallowed. "No, but it was a near thing."

He forced himself to relax his hands. "Does this sort of reaction happen often?" *Another stupid question, Morgan. It's none of your business.*

"God, I hope not."

"Did I do something that scared you? Tell me, Rachel. Was it something I did?"

She gave him a sad smile. "You kissed me."

The pained expression on Jared's face might have been funny under other circumstances.

"No," Rachel cried, reaching for him. "I didn't mean it like that. I wanted you to kiss me. You didn't do anything wrong, Jared. I didn't know this would happen. You're the first . . . I mean, I haven't . . . I . . . I didn't know this would happen."

He took her trembling hand in his and studied it intently. What she'd just told him, without actually saying it, was that he was the first man she'd kissed since someone had nearly raped her. He'd been so intent on his own pleasure, he hadn't worried about being gentle. He'd let his hunger for her get control and fog his brain. "I feel like such a bastard."

"And I feel like a total fool."

"You have nothing to feel foolish about. What happened was not your fault."

"It wasn't yours either, Jared."

Logically, Jared might someday be able to convince himself of that. Someone from Rachel's past had traumatized her, attacked her, nearly raped her. The rage that surged through Jared at the thought made him want to find the man responsible and make him pay.

But when he looked around the room, the only man present was Jared Morgan. No matter what she said, he would always blame himself for that look of terror in her eyes.

"Jared," Rachel said, "I mean it. It wasn't your fault. Please don't blame yourself."

Jared brought her hand to his lips and kissed her knuckles. "Get some rest. If you want to skip the meeting tomorrow—"

"No. I'll be fine."

So she said. But he wondered.

When the phone rang at seven the next morning, Rachel shot straight up, surprised to realize she'd actually fallen asleep sometime during the night. She answered the wake-up call, then lost any semblance of alertness. Groggy from only a few hours of sleep, she groped her way through the darkness to the bathroom.

She flipped on the light, then groaned as a thousand needles of pain shot into her eyes. Two giant hammers took up a rhythmic pounding inside her head. A glance at the mirror confirmed that she looked as bad as she felt.

She'd spent most of the night shivering in the aftermath of her panic, tossing and turning, trying to forget. Sutton, Hank, Jared, Jared's mother. The world's longest elevator ride. The world's most disastrous dinner. The world's most devastating kiss. The terror that had followed. There were a lot of things to forget.

Jared's kiss had been so sweet, so hot. And then she had panicked. *Damn you, Carl Sutton, what have you done to me?*

How was she ever going to face Jared again?

I won't, she told herself. At least, she wouldn't face him again the way she had last night—without her disguise, her protection.

He hired a bag lady, and that's what he was going to get. If he wanted a fashion model, he could damn well find one somewhere else. If he wanted a normal woman who could share a simple kiss without going berserk, he'd have to look elsewhere for her too.

With her mind made up, Rachel showered, then resumed her hated disguise. It was still early when she was dressed and ready to go. She didn't want to wait for Jared. She'd rather face him in a conference room full of people than here, alone, in her room.

Jared stepped from the shower, tucked the towel around his waist, and frowned at his blurred image in the steamy mirror.

What the hell had happened last night? Had that really been Rachel? Was that gorgeous creature with a body that would make a monk break his vows really his secretary? Had he held her? Kissed her? Had she really responded to him in a way no woman had before? And now that her disguise was out of the way . . . now what? Go on as before? As if nothing had changed?

But something *had* changed. Last night they'd crossed a barrier he'd never crossed with someone who worked for him, but it was a barrier he'd gladly cross again—with Rachel.

Rachel.

He closed his eyes and pictured her as she'd been last night, all golden and soft and desirable.

It was a full minute before he remembered how the night had ended. He swore at himself viciously. He should have known better, dammit. The disguise, the fear in her eyes when he'd discovered her deception, her halfhearted explanation of the wig and glasses. He should have known it was more serious than that.

He looked in the mirror again, and his mouth quirked up at one corner. *What now, Morgan? You gonna chase her around the desk?*

He sneered at his reflection. No, he wasn't going to chase her around the desk. He knew that. But right now, that was about all he knew, except that he didn't want to think about not ever being able to kiss her again. He would just have to take things as they came.

With a troubled sigh he reached for his shaving kit. Something white flashed in the mirror. He poked his head out the bathroom door and saw a piece of paper on the floor, just inside the door to the hall.

Puzzled, he walked over and picked it up. It was Rachel's handwriting. *Jared: I got ready early, so I'll meet you in the conference room. Rachel.*

Dammit, he'd hoped to talk to her before the meeting.

Just then he heard a door close out in the hall, and without thinking, he went to his door and stepped out.

• • •

Rachel punched the elevator button, then pushed the hated green glasses up on her nose. A door opened down the hall, and she turned toward the sound. Her eyes widened at the sight of Jared standing outside his room wearing nothing but a frustrated frown and a damp towel.

All she could do was stare. After last night, she half expected to feel panic clawing at her throat. Instead, she felt heat, and it wasn't in her throat. The sight of all that dark curly hair across his chest, glistening with moisture and narrowing to a thin line that disappeared beneath the towel, did strange things to her pulse.

He took a step toward her, and she swallowed.

"Dammit, Rachel."

Just then another door opened down the hall, and two elderly ladies stepped from their room. They were so engrossed in their conversation that they were only ten feet from Jared before they noticed him.

"Mildred," said the woman in the flaming-orange polyester pantsuit.

"Yes," answered her friend in radioactive yellow. "Did you ever see so much glorious black hair? And so straight and silky-looking."

As they walked past Jared, their eyes cut to him while they faced straight ahead.

"Mildred," the first one said, keeping her voice low, but not low enough. "I do believe you need new glasses. His hair is as curly as can be."

"Oh, dear." Mildred blushed. "I must confess, dear, I was looking at his legs."

The two passed Rachel at the elevator and kept walking.

"Well, if we're confessing," the first woman said, "I'm afraid I was looking at his chest."

For a moment Jared was too stunned to do more than stand and stare. Then, with a jerk, he stepped back into his room, choking on startled laughter and fighting a chest-to-scalp blush. He gave a final peek down the hall just in time to see Rachel step into the elevator, trailing strangled laughter in her wake.

By the time Rachel reached the conference room, she was still smiling. At least those two little old ladies had allowed her to make a clean getaway. And bless them, they'd taken her mind off last night.

A few minutes later all thoughts of the incident in the hall and of last night fled as she readied the room for the upcoming meeting. She made certain each place at the long table had a legal pad, pen, and glass of ice water. Coffee and doughnuts in the far corner.

She noticed there was no orange juice. Jared would want his orange juice. After ordering some, she proceeded to set up her tape recorder.

Her main function, as Jared had described it, was to take notes of the meeting and pass out the appropriate reports at the appropriate time.

The recorder would eliminate the need to write down every word that was spoken, but she'd still have to take notes, since she didn't know these people and wouldn't be able to tell who was who by listening to their voices.

Remembering all the work she and Jared had done over the last few weeks, she mentally crossed her fingers that all would go well for him during the next couple of days.

The door to the hall opened, and Rachel turned. Instead of the waiter with the orange juice, it was Jared. She straightened her spine and met his gaze, refusing to let what had happened last night control her any further. She couldn't let it interfere with her job. She wouldn't let her past rob her of a future.

A brief picture of the two ladies in the hall destroyed her calm look. Her hand flew to her mouth, but not before a giggle escaped.

One corner of Jared's mouth twitched. "Good morning to you too." He pushed his jacket back and stuffed his hands in his pants pockets as he strolled over to stand in front of her.

His smile faded. "Are you all right?"

"I'm fine." She made herself hold his gaze. "If it's all the same to you, I'd just as soon not talk about last night."

"Pretend it never happened?"

"Exactly."

"All of it?" he asked softly.

Rachel felt heat sting her cheeks. "Considering the way it ended, I think that's best."

His shoulders rose and fell on a deep breath. "As long as you realize I never meant to hurt you," he said. "I would never intentionally cause you pain, Rachel. I hope you believe that."

Rachel swallowed. "I do."

A moment passed, then his eyes narrowed and looked her up and down, spending an undue amount of time on her wig and glasses. Rachel lost all urge to laugh. It was plain by the look on his face that he didn't approve of her being back in disguise today. His next words confirmed it.

"You look like hell."

Rachel stiffened. "You never seemed to mind before how I looked."

Jared shrugged. "Actually, I was referring to the dark circles under your eyes. But now that you mention it—" Before she could stop him, he reached up and removed her glasses. "At least don't ruin your eyes by looking through these damn things."

Rachel made a grab for the glasses, but he moved away and tucked them into his jacket pocket. Any reply she might have made was cut off when a waiter came in carrying a large bowl filled with crushed ice and small plastic jugs of orange juice.

"Sorry about the oversight, ma'am," the waiter said. "I'll be sure and have it here in the morning."

As he set the bowl down next to the doughnuts, three other men entered the room and called out greetings to Jared. When everyone had arrived, Jared introduced Rachel to his fellow general managers. She noticed some of them giving Jared strange looks, and two men even smirked when she was introduced.

Rachel bristled. How dare these men judge her solely on her looks? She began to develop a strong empathy for plain-looking women everywhere.

The man named Holt, from Salt Lake City, punched Jared in the arm and laughed. "What happened to the lady in gold I saw you get off the elevator with last night, Morgan?"

Rachel, who had her back to the two men, stiffened.

"I wish I knew, Holt. I wish I knew."

Rachel clenched her teeth and shot Jared a murderous look.

"You mean she got away?" Holt demanded.

Jared grinned. "Only temporarily, my friend. I'll find her again. You can bet on it."

Before Rachel could do or say anything stupid, Harve Kennedy, the corporation's president of broadcasting, called the meeting to order.

At first Rachel took notes fast and furiously, until she became more familiar with the different voices her recorder was capturing. One voice in particular she knew she'd have no trouble recognizing: Jared's. Every time he spoke, she had trouble concentrating.

She did manage to pay attention, however, when Jared mentioned his proposed program change. That was one of the things they'd researched for days. He'd said he wanted enough statistics to back up his rather unorthodox request.

Harve Kennedy looked at Jared skeptically, then glanced at his watch. "I assume you're prepared to argue your case," he said with a smile. When Jared smiled back and nodded, Harve continued, "Then let's break for lunch and take it up as soon as we get back."

The men rose from the table on cue, and some of them headed for the door immediately, as if they couldn't wait to get out.

When Cynthia Morgan came in to go to lunch with Jared, Rachel wanted to crawl into a hole and hide. *Please don't let her see me.*

Rachel circled the table, keeping her back to the door as much as possible, and emptied ashtrays and gathered empty coffee cups to avoid going anywhere near the door until Jared and his mother left.

The murmur of voices died down, and she let herself relax. Too soon.

"Rachel?"

At the sound of his voice right behind her, she cringed.

"Rachel," he repeated, a definite note of laughter in his voice.

Slowly, she turned around to face him. It was as she'd feared. Cynthia was standing there, her mouth hanging open in shock. Her head pivoted back and forth as she looked from Jared to Rachel and back again. When her gaze returned to Rachel the third time, recognition dawned. Her eyes widened.

Jared smiled at his mother, then shrugged. To Rachel he said, "We're going for lunch. Would you like to join us?"

Rachel tried to swallow, but her mouth was too dry. "Uh, no. No thank you. I've . . . got some things I need to do."

He pursed his lips to keep from laughing. "All right. I'll see you later, coward. Come on, Mother. Let's eat. I'm starved."

As the couple went through the doorway, Rachel heard Cynthia whisper, "Jared Morgan, you tell me what's going on, and you tell me right this minute."

Jared's answering laughter rang down the hall.

Afraid to stick her head out the door, Rachel had room service bring her a sandwich.

When the meeting resumed an hour later, Jared had the floor.

"What I want to do, Harve, is drop the late-night network programming and run a local movie."

"You know the network is going to scream at a move like that," Harve said.

"Let them scream," Jared said. "Until they provide me with a program that will attract at least a *few* viewers, I'm wasting airtime and money."

Jared went on to explain his plan, then leaned back in his chair and caught Rachel's eyes with his. He gave her a big wink.

Hal Holt saw and nearly choked on a mouthful of coffee.

The rest of the afternoon passed in a blur for Rachel as she took notes and tried to keep up with what was going on. A lot of what the men discussed was still foreign to her, but Jared would be able to answer any questions she had.

Jared.

She hoped Harve would let him try out his idea of a late-night movie. She hoped it would work, that the Oklahoma City viewers would like the idea.

And she hoped that somehow, by some miracle, she and Jared could regain their easy, friendly working relationship.

When the meeting was over, Harve announced that the company was picking up the tab for dinner and a show later that night. Rachel, too, was included in the invitation, and for a moment panic set in. There was no way she could spend a sociable evening in Jared's company. Not after last night. Not even dressed as she was.

Then she remembered the typing she'd planned to do tonight and realized with relief that she had a legitimate excuse to decline.

As the men left the room a short time later, Jared hung around until he and Rachel were the only two left. She moved around the room, straightening this, fiddling with that, trying to look busy, hoping he'd leave. He didn't. Instead, he stalked her, and finally cornered her next to the coffeepot.

"Pretending last night didn't happen was your idea. Why do I get the distinct feeling you're trying to avoid me?" he asked, his voice low and deceptively pleasant.

Unless she turned toward the wall, there was no

place for Rachel to look but at Jared. She focused on the knot of his tie. "Don't be silly. Of course I'm not trying to avoid you."

The knot bobbed up, then down, as Jared swallowed. "We have to talk, you know."

"About what?" *Dumb! Dumb, dumb, dumb!* How could she be so stupid as to give him an opening like that? One he was sure to take advantage of.

Which he did. "About last night. About you. About me. About where we go from here."

While he stood there, so relaxed it was disgusting, Rachel side-stepped around him and began gathering her recorder, notepad, and purse. "Is that all?" she asked, her voice all business. "I'm the secretary. You're the boss. From here, you go to dinner and a show, and I go to the computer."

Just as she was about to make it out the door, he stopped her with a hand on her shoulder. A warm, firm hand that made her spine tingle.

"And last night?"

Rachel forced herself to pull out of his grasp and turn to face him. "Last night was a mistake. A rather disastrous one, I'm sure you'll agree, that won't be repeated."

She turned away and headed for the elevator as fast as she could without actually running. Her knees felt watery, and her heart pounded. She didn't take a breath until she found herself inside the closed elevator—without Jared.

The only thing Rachel was pleased about during the second day of meetings was that Jared received permission to run his late-night movies during the July rating period. It gave her a sense of satisfaction to know she'd helped him gather the information needed to convince Harve it was a good idea. She'd even helped Jared and the program director, Ben Davidson, select movie titles from the station's film library—that was the part she'd liked the best during all those late nights of work.

Once Harve okayed Jared's plans, Rachel spent the rest of the time staying on the opposite side of the room from Jared and avoiding looking at him. When the meeting ended that afternoon, some of the men planned to stay over one more night, but Rachel and Jared had plane reservations for that evening. She'd just finished packing when Jared knocked on her door. On her way to open it she wiped her sweaty palms on her skirt.

"Are you ready?"

Rachel nodded, and Jared, saying he'd rather not wait for a bellman, picked up his luggage, then came into her room and got hers. "Let's go home," he said.

Rachel had been dreading the flight home for nothing. As it turned out, Jared made no attempt at personal conversation, and she dozed, or pretended to, most of the time.

Their plane landed a few minutes ahead of schedule, and when no one met Rachel at the gate, Jared insisted on staying with her until her ride arrived. She nearly panicked, fearing she'd have to introduce him to Mike. She still hadn't gotten around to mentioning she had two children, and at this point, it would be a bit awkward.

They stood just inside the doors at the downstairs baggage-claim area and waited. A few minutes later Rachel spotted Mike pulling up outside.

"Here's my ride. You didn't need to stay with me, but thank you anyway." Without waiting for a response, she threw a "See you tomorrow" over her shoulder and ran to the car before Mike could even get out.

Jared stood where he was and watched her leave. He couldn't see the driver of the car well, but it was a man. His eyes narrowed. What kind of game was she playing? And why did that car look familiar? It wasn't one he remembered seeing parked at the station, but it was still familiar somehow. There weren't that many 1965 fire-engine-red rag-top Mustangs around these days. Especially ones in mint condition. With Missouri tags.

More questions to add to the puzzle of Rachel Fredrick. And he fully intended to get some answers. Soon.

The rest of that week and all of the next were hectic at the station. It was the second Friday after Las Vegas before Rachel had a chance to slow down long enough to catch her breath.

She blew on her coffee to cool it and wandered past her desk to look out her office window. The sights were familiar to her now. The yellow daffodils and white, gold, and lavender irises blooming in the carefully tended flower beds along the sidewalks and parking lot. The clumps of love grass in the field beyond. The sumac, in full leaf now. The blackjack trees, the last to release winter, still a new spring green. The giant transmitting towers of Channel 3 and the other stations, with their alternating red and white sections reaching up to tickle the bellies of fluffy white clouds. The taillights of Jared's car as it rounded the last bend in the drive, then pulled out onto Britton Road.

Rachel let the mini-blinds flop back in place and returned to her desk with a feeling of relief.

Three o'clock. Monday, Wednesday, and Friday. Freedom. Those were the times she was free of Jared Morgan. At least physically.

He never volunteered where he went three afternoons each week, and she didn't dare ask.

These days she barely dared to breathe around him. She was walking on eggshells, and he was stomping around, growling like a bear with a sore paw. Every time he looked at her wig or her clothes, disapproval showed in his heavy frown.

And every time it happened, Rachel stuck her chin in the air and glared right back—without the concealing safety of her glasses, which he had kept.

But when he looked in her eyes . . . oh, God. His eyes could make her bones melt. And it scared the hell out of her.

She'd been waiting ever since their return from Las Vegas. Over two weeks now. Waiting for she wasn't sure what. A confrontation. More questions maybe, or demands. Something. Anything! Anything but his quiet looks. Contemplating looks that said, *I remember that kiss . . . do you?*

Hot looks that said, *I want to feel your body next to mine again.*

Intense looks that said, *Please don't be afraid of me.*

Soft looks. *Talk to me. Trust me.*

Daring looks. *Forget what happened in your past. Remember how much you liked kissing me.*

Challenging looks. *Try to forget that my hands have touched you, my lips have kissed you. And you touched and kissed me back. Go ahead. Try to forget. I dare you.*

She shivered at the memory of that look. She couldn't possibly forget the way his hands felt, the taste of him.

Neither could she forget her fears. So many fears. If all she had to deal with was the panic she'd felt, she honestly thought she could cope.

But she didn't know how to cope with the rest. Being attacked by a maniac wasn't the worst that had happened to her five years ago. She closed her eyes and saw his face, imagined she could feel the gun in her hand.

No. She would not think of it. It was over.

But Sutton's attack was nothing compared to Hank's betrayal. Hank, her loving husband, father of her children, hadn't believed Sutton had attacked her. "He wouldn't have bothered," Hank had said. "I'd already told him the truth about you."

Confused, devastated, Rachel had asked what he'd meant.

"I told him that in bed, you were . . . disappointing, at best."

A cold shudder ripped through her. Just the memory of those words, of the disgust in Hank's eyes, was enough to destroy what peace of mind she'd managed to gain during the past five years.

Never, never, would she open herself up to that kind of pain and humiliation again. Of all the secrets from her past, that one was the most devastating.

No, there would never be anything between her and Jared. Never.

"Rachel? You okay?"

Rachel blinked. The memories dissolved. Bobby Johnson, the page, stood in her doorway. She smiled. "I'm fine. Just thinking, that's all."

"Well, quit thinking so hard," Bobby said with a laugh. "It's Friday, it's five o'clock, and it's springtime. Time to get outta this place."

Rachel pulled open her bottom drawer and

grabbed her purse. "Right you are, Mr. Johnson. And I've got someplace I'm supposed to be. See you Monday."

The "someplace" was Caroline's softball game. It was the season opener for the girls' slow-pitch inner-city league, and Rachel had promised her daughter she'd be there.

Mike was waiting at the curb when she walked outside. He took her home, where she ditched her wig and put on a bra that fit rather than strangled. She climbed into jeans and a sweatshirt, then she and Mike headed for the game.

Wheeler Park was located in a not-too-wonderful part of town, on Western, just south of Interstate 40.

"How will we ever find her?" asked Rachel, looking out at three separate games in progress on three separate diamonds. "Are we late?"

"No," Mike said. "Hers is the second game on this first field."

Mike parked the Mustang, and by the time he and Rachel reached the small, crowded bleachers, Caroline was there to meet them. She was jumping from foot to foot, tugging on various parts of her new blue-and-gold uniform.

"Wow, you guys, you just barely made it. This game's about over, and we're up next. Gotta run!"

Rachel smiled and shook her head at her daughter's retreating back. "Nice to see you too, kid," she mumbled.

By the time Rachel and Mike bought soft drinks and hot dogs, a double play ended the game on the field, and over half the people in the stands headed for the parking area.

While eating her hot dog, Rachel watched Caroline's team huddle around a tall man with dark wavy hair and broad shoulders. Must be their coach. The "hunk" Caroline was always talking about.

The way he stood, relaxed, hands on hips, reminded her of Jared. He was the right height, the right build . . . good grief, it *was* Jared! She'd never seen him in anything other than a suit, except for that time he'd been wearing nothing but a towel. Her cheeks flushed at the memory.

Yes, that was Jared Morgan on the field, all right. She'd recognize that tush anywhere. The very thought made her cheeks sting hotter.

What was he doing here? Heaven help her! If he was Caroline's coach, he was also Caroline's best friend's father.

The gods must be laughing their heads off. Here she'd been trying her best to keep her distance from Jared, and now their lives were more intertwined than ever.

Well, it wasn't going to matter. She couldn't let it.

She forced her gaze away and concentrated on the opposing team warming up out on the field. But no matter how she tried, her gaze kept straying back to Jared.

She choked down the last bite of her hot dog just as the opposing team cleared the field, allowing Caroline's Bluejays their turn at warming up.

Rachel wondered frantically if she could somehow hide. But no, she couldn't do that. When he saw her, and he would, she knew, she would simply have to face him.

Five

"Come on, you laggards, get into position," Jared hollered. The outfield was ready and waiting, while his own daughter, Deb, and her best friend, Caro Harding, ambled slowly into the infield. He popped a fly to left field and groaned when Susan missed it. "Wake up out there!"

"Did your mom make it, Caro?" Deb's voice floated back to Jared while Susan picked up the ball and threw it to third base.

"Yeah, she made it, finally," Caro answered.

Deb turned around and walked backward so she faced the stands. "Which one is she?"

"The one with the long blond hair, sitting next to my brother, Mike."

Jared popped another fly, this one to right field. When the bat connected with the ball, something clicked in his brain.

Long blond hair. Brother. Mike. Fire-engine-red 1965 rag-top Mustang.

It couldn't be.

Jared spun toward the stands and had to shade the sun from his eyes with his hand. It couldn't be her. It just couldn't be. He wasn't that lucky.

He scanned the faces in the stands, anxious,

hopeful. He spotted Mike Harding in the middle of the third row. And next to him, staring back at him, just as stunned as he was—Rachel. Not the Rachel he saw every day at work, not the coolly glamorous Rachel he'd met one night in Las Vegas, not the terrified Rachel who had panicked in his arms. This was the real Rachel, the smiling, outgoing, friendly, soft, beautiful Rachel. The one he'd been wanting to meet. *Rachel.*

He caught the look of shock on her face and grinned. *Well, well, well. Rachel.*

"Look out, Coach!"

"Dad!"

Jared turned and ducked just in time to avoid getting hit square in the ear with the returning ball—the one he should have been expecting, except that all his attention had been focused on Rachel.

Even with his near miss, he couldn't wipe the grin off his face. *Now I know what the term "knockout" means, when applied to a woman.*

"At this rate," Mike grumbled beside Rachel, "the Bluejays are bound to lose. You know him?"

Rachel's eyes never left Jared as the game got under way. She answered Mike in a distracted voice. "He's my boss."

"Your what?"

Rachel focused on Mike and shrugged. "Jared Morgan is my boss."

"At the television station?"

"That's the one."

"But . . . but . . . he recognized you! Without your wig and stuff."

Rachel glanced away. "He, uh, saw me without it in Las Vegas."

"How'd that happen?"

"Just one of those things," Rachel hedged. "It

was an accident. A mistake on my part. Anyway, it happened."

"What'd he say when he found out? And if he already knows, how come you keep up the costume? He must hate it. I know you do."

Rachel squirmed in her seat. What could she say? She couldn't very well tell her son that she kept up her disguise as a barrier against a man she shouldn't be attracted to but was. A flimsy barrier, at that.

She was saved from answering when Caroline put a runner out on second and Mike jumped up to shout, "Way to go, Caro!"

A few minutes later the center fielder caught a fly ball for the third out, and the Bluejays started in from the field for their turn at bat. Jared strolled over to the backstop and looked up at Rachel, a slow smile spreading across his face.

"Hi, Mike," he said, his eyes still on Rachel. His gaze roamed slowly over every inch of her, touching her, warming her, stealing her breath. In a voice as thick and slow as molasses, he said, "Good to . . . see you."

Rachel felt Mike stiffen beside her. If Jared didn't stop staring at her that way, as if she were his own personal property, there was liable to be trouble. Rachel felt certain that if she looked up the word "overprotective" in the dictionary, her son's picture would be there in place of the usual definition.

Finally, Jared pulled his gaze away and looked at Mike with a grin and a wink. "Nice mom you've got there, Harding."

Before Mike could answer, Jared turned and joined his team on the bench that took the place of a dugout.

From somewhere down in front a laughing female voice floated up: "The season sure won't be dull with her around. Did you see the way Morgan looked at her? I'd sell my kids for a look like that from a man like him."

"If *that's* how he looks at you, no wonder you keep your disguise," Mike said, his eyes narrowed to slits as he stared a hole in Jared's back. "Does he know everything?"

Rachel took her first full breath in minutes, then let it out slowly. "No. Apparently he was out of the country when, well, you know. He didn't know who I was."

As the first Bluejay waited for the pitch, Mike asked, "So what're ya gonna do?"

She shrugged. "That's up to him. I won't quit my job. Not unless I have to. All he'd have to do would be to tell the employment agency what I've done. I'd never get another job in this city."

Mike brooded for a while, then surprised Rachel with, "You want me to have a talk with him?"

Her first impulse was to cry. He was so grown-up. Almost a man now, no longer a little boy. She swallowed her tears and gave him a hug. "Thanks, honey, but no. It'll be all right. You'll see."

From the other end of the stands, halfway to third base, a boy cried out, "Hey, Harding! Who's that baby doll ya got hanging all over ya?"

Rachel cringed, feeling her cheeks heat up. Jared must have heard—everybody else certainly had—for he turned to look at her, then seemed to search the stands for the voice that had called out.

Mike put his arm around Rachel's shoulders, then cupped his other hand to his mouth. "My mother, you idiot!"

"Michael!" Rachel admonished.

Laughter from at least two dozen witnesses made her cheeks sting. The talkative woman in the front row said, "See? It's gonna be an interesting season."

The game ended minutes, hours, maybe years, later. Rachel couldn't have said which. The Bluejays won their season opener, 12 to 7. Amid the cheers and applause, Rachel caught a masculine snicker from a few rows behind.

"Yeah, well," a voice said, "you can have ol' what's-his-face's mother. Me, I got my eye on that little yellow-headed shortstop just coming in off the field. What a little fox, huh?"

Rachel stood slowly and turned toward the voice. She spotted him at once, since he was still laughing. Nineteen, maybe twenty years old—too old to be hanging around young girls. Greasy jeans, a torn T-shirt that said SCUBA DIVERS DO IT DEEPER, a gold loop dangling from a pierced ear, and a three-inch-tall pink mohawk.

The blood in Rachel's veins turned cold, then hot. The punk and his buddy, who was also no prize in Rachel's eyes—young men with greasy ponytails never were, especially ones whose flabby stomachs hung down over their belts and jiggled grossly with every step—started down the bleachers. Intent on reaching the field of girls, neither one saw Rachel until she stepped in front of them.

"Just a minute, mister," she said, her voice hard.

Mohawk grinned, revealing yellowed front teeth, one of which was chipped.

"Hot damn," his friend muttered. "You always was luckier than me."

Mike took a step closer to his mother, but

Rachel motioned him back. She glared at the one who'd just spoken, then focused on Mohawk again. "That 'little fox' you're talking about happens to be only twelve years old."

Mohawk's grin widened. He took a step closer to Rachel. She tossed her hair back and stood her ground. "And if that isn't enough to change your mind, then try this: She's also my daughter. If you get within ten feet of her—"

Mohawk opened his mouth to say something, then shut it with an audible snap. A strong, warm hand settled on Rachel's shoulder, and a deep, familiar voice asked, "Any trouble here?"

Rachel nearly sagged with relief when she heard Jared's voice. She didn't know what she would have done if the punk had tried anything, but she wasn't about to let him anywhere near her daughter.

"No," she said, her voice cool, her eyes still locked on Mohawk. "These . . . *gentlemen* were just leaving."

Ponytail took a step away from Jared. "Hey, Scooter, come on, man, let's split."

Scooter looked as if he might want to push the issue. He glanced from Mike to Rachel and smirked. Then he looked at Jared. Scooter's smirk disappeared, and he stepped back. He gave a nervous laugh, then followed his friend and left the bleachers.

The reassuring hand on Rachel's shoulder tightened and jerked her around to face a furious Jared.

"That was a damn fool thing to do, taking on two creeps like that. You could have got yourself hurt."

Rachel winced at the ache in her shoulder, and he loosened his grip somewhat. "Thanks for your concern, but I knew what I was doing. I could have handled it."

"Could have handled it!" Jared turned her loose and threw his hands up in the air. He took a step nearer, until he towered over her. He bent down until his nose was a mere inch from hers. "And just how were you going to *handle* it if those two had decided to jump you?"

It never dawned on Rachel, in that moment when Jared loomed over her like a giant menace, to fear for her safety. At least not until she felt Mike inch closer to her side, and she caught a glimpse of his pale, drawn face. Was he upset about what Jared said or by Jared's seemingly threatening pose?

In either case Rachel knew *she* wasn't afraid. Not of Jared. Not physically. Her sense of relief was so great, she wanted to dance and shout. He had grabbed her, jerked her around, and yelled at her, and she hadn't panicked.

She put her arm around Mike's shoulder and let a wry grin twist the corner of her mouth. "He's right, you know," she told her son. "It really was pretty stupid of me."

From the corner of her eye she saw a thousand questions flit across Jared's face as he watched the play between her and Mike.

Just then Caroline showed up, bringing another girl with her, whom she introduced to Rachel as Deb, her best friend. Both girls were still high on the evening's victory.

"Mrs. Harding," said Deb, green eyes sparkling. "Can Caro come over and spend the night?"

Rachel stiffened at being called Mrs. Harding, but said nothing. It was a natural mistake for Deb to assume Caroline and her mother had the same last name.

"Please, Mom, please?" Caroline pleaded.

"Well, I don't know," Rachel said hesitantly. "What do your parents say, Deb?"

"Dad already said it was okay." Deb sidled up to Jared and put her arm around his waist. "Didn't ya, Dad?" she said, looking up at him with adoring eyes.

Dad. Of course. Rachel knew the coach was the father of Caro's best friend. She had acknowledged that fact earlier when she first recognized Jared. Still, she'd have to get used to it.

"Sure did," Jared answered, giving his daughter a wink.

Rachel blinked. "You're my daughter's best friend's father."

Jared grinned and shrugged. "Small world, isn't it?"

"Wait a minute," Caroline said, looking from one parent to the other. "You mean you two know each other?"

When Jared explained that Rachel was his secretary, both girls looked stunned. A moment later they looked at each other, and slow grins spread across sweaty freckled faces.

"My mother works for your father!" Caroline cried, laughing.

"It's the greatest!" Deb shouted.

Caroline suddenly grabbed Deb's arm, her eyes wide. "Do you realize what this means? It means we're—"

"Practically related!" Deb finished.

Both girls squealed, then jumped up and down while trying to hug each other. Jared laughed; Rachel gave a nervous chuckle; Mike rolled his eyes to heaven, as if silently praying for deliverance from the antics of twelve-year-old girls.

"Can I spend the night, Mom? Can I?"

"Well, I don't—"

"Aw, come on, Mom," Caroline pleaded.

"Yeah," said Jared, still laughing. "Come on, Mom."

When Jared offered to stop by their house on the way home so Caroline could pick up some clean clothes, Rachel finally agreed. Caroline needed to develop this friendship, Rachel knew. She just wished it could have been with someone other than her boss's daughter, for heaven's sake.

"In honor of tonight's victory," said Jared, his eyes scanning the small group, "why don't we stop off for pizza on the way? My treat."

Both girls squealed again. Rachel didn't have the heart to spoil things, so she agreed to go along with Jared's plan. When they reached the parking lot and Jared asked Mike to take the girls with him so he could talk to Rachel, her easy mood vanished.

Her mind scurried, trying to think of an excuse to avoid being alone with Jared. The next thing she knew, a long look passed between Jared and Mike, a look of questions, a look of answers. Whatever it was, Mike seemed satisfied with what he saw. In the blink of an eye he abandoned his mother and herded the two jabbering twelve-year-olds toward the Mustang, leaving Rachel and Jared standing beside his Lincoln in the otherwise-empty parking lot.

Neither one spoke until Jared cleared his throat a few minutes later as he pulled out onto the interstate. "So," he said. "You're Caro's mother."

Rachel stared at his hands clutching the steering wheel and suddenly realized he was as nervous about this as she was. The knowledge allowed her to relax somewhat.

"Caro looks so much like you it's amazing. But Mike," he said, shaking his head. "You're not old enough to have a son Mike's age. Gypsies leave him on your doorstep?"

Rachel laughed and relaxed another degree. "I think maybe there was a compliment in there somewhere. But he's mine, all right."

After a moment of easy silence Jared asked, "And are you Mrs. Harding? Is there a Mr. Harding?"

Rachel swallowed, her easiness evaporating. "I took back my maiden name. I'm divorced."

Jared's hands relaxed completely on the steering wheel, and he smiled. "Me too."

"And you have custody?"

His smile twisted. "My ex didn't want to be tied down—by either of us."

Rachel bit her lip on any more questions about his divorce, but another matter occurred to her. "Mike and Caroline understand why I don't want anyone to know who I am, so they don't talk about me," she said. "But how is it that Caroline didn't know you're the general manager of Channel 3? I'd think that would be a major topic of conversation among twelve-year-old girls."

"That's Deb's doing," he answered, turning off I-40 and heading north on I-44. "She had some problems the last place we lived with girls making friends with her, hoping she could get them on television or some such nonsense. I think she'd done a bit of bragging or something. Anyway, she got hurt. She's pretty quiet about what I do for a living since we moved here."

"Well, at least now I know what you do on those afternoons you disappear from the office. Any particular reason you never mentioned it?"

"What?" Jared cried with mock dismay. "And

have you find out I was out cavorting in the sunshine while you had to slave away at work? I've got more sense than that."

Rachel laughed. "I don't know how much sense you can have if you think coaching those girls is the same as cavorting. It's hard work, and you know it."

"I don't mind," he said with a shrug. "I like doing it."

Rachel was silent then as Jared followed the Mustang and exited the interstate onto Northwest Expressway. At the stoplight she felt his eyes on her as if they were touching her. "You're staring."

"I know," he said softly. "I can't help it. I like looking at you. This is only the second time I've ever really seen you, you know."

"No," she said, catching his gaze and holding it. "This is the first time you've ever seen me. That other person was someone else . . . someone I used to be. *This* is who I am. Jeans, sweatshirts, and two children."

Jared gripped the steering wheel harder. It was all he could do to keep from reaching out to stroke that long golden curl that lay across her shoulder. He wanted to feel the soft silkiness against his skin. Wanted to touch her cheek. Taste her lips. Hear her sigh. But he didn't want to scare her.

He turned and focused on the Mustang's taillights, concentrating, trying to ease the sudden tightness in his loins. There was no way he could get out of the car in this condition.

His grip tightened even more on the steering wheel, until his knuckles turned white. He tried thinking of unpleasant things: a losing softball season; low ratings for his new movie; low ratings in general; a strike in the newsroom; four-foot chunks of ice falling from the tower onto the roof of his car some winter. None of those things helped.

What cooled his blood was the fear that if he ever got the chance to kiss Rachel again, she would panic as she had before. He wondered if her ex-husband was the bastard responsible.

Jared parked behind Mike and got out without asking any of the questions in his mind. He had agreed to pretend that night in Las Vegas never happened. He would go along with her wishes. For now.

Caro and Deb were still wound up with excitement, and they entered the restaurant first, followed immediately by Mike. When Rachel reached the door, Jared grabbed her hand and stopped her on the sidewalk. "Rachel?"

She looked up at him, and he read hesitancy and uncertainty in her gaze. *Easy, Morgan*, he cautioned himself. *Don't push too fast. Don't scare her off.* But damn, it was hard, when all he wanted to do was hold her, feel her body pressed against his, feel the soft yielding of her lips.

He gripped her fingers tightly and cleared his throat. "Is it possible for us to be friends, you and me?"

Her eyes widened. "Friends? Is that what you want?"

He felt the moistness of her palm, the trembling of her fingers. At least he wasn't the only nervous one around here. "Yes," he answered. "Friends. I want more than that, but for now, friends will do. What do you say?"

"I'm . . . not interested in anything beyond friendship."

Liar, he thought, reading the look in her eyes. He smiled then. "Fair enough. Friends?"

After a moment Rachel nodded. "Friends."

Jared breathed a sigh of relief and held the door open. One hurdle crossed.

The kids had taken over a round corner booth, with Caroline seated in the middle. Rachel slid in next to Mike, so Jared sat beside Deb.

"Can me and Caro watch MTV on the big screen, Dad?"

"I don't believe I heard that," Jared said, one brow cocked.

Deb grinned at him. "May Caroline and I please watch MTV on the big screen tonight, Father?"

Jared returned her grin. "Yes, you may."

Caroline squealed. "Did you hear that, Mom? A big screen! And MTV! Wow!"

"I heard, I heard."

When the waitress came to take their order, it took several minutes to straighten out who liked which toppings. When asked about drinks, Jared said, "I'll have a beer."

"The same for me," said Rachel, eliciting his surprise.

"Me too!" chimed in three other voices.

Jared and Rachel both gave mock glares to their grinning children. "That's beer for the adults," Jared told the waitress, "and a soft drink of their choice for the children."

Deb and Caro both groaned and rolled their eyes. Mike, however, wore a smug, superior look, until Rachel spoke up.

"All *three* children."

Jared stretched back in the booth and crossed his arms over his chest as he let the conversation the other four were having drift around him.

This was the Rachel he'd longed to know. This

easygoing, smiling, laughing, vibrant, sexy Rachel. How could a woman look so poised, so utterly desirable, with a string of cheese dangling from her lips? It was all he could do to keep from leaning across the table and swiping at that cheese with his tongue.

When her own tongue flicked out to capture it, he almost groaned aloud. He forced his gaze away from her glistening lips and tried to concentrate on his food. What was he eating, anyway?

Oh, yeah. Pizza. In front of his daughter, and Caro. And Mike. He'd have to watch himself around Mike. The boy acted more like an overprotective older brother than like Rachel's son.

And the boy was sharp. Maybe too sharp. If Jared wasn't careful, Mike would be asking him what his intentions were.

And that was one question Jared didn't want to think about.

All he knew was that Rachel Fredrick fascinated him. He wanted to get to know her. Wanted to get close to her. Close enough that she would never know fear again. And if the truth be known, he just plain wanted her. Wanted her the way he'd never wanted another woman.

The next day Rachel congratulated herself on getting a good night's sleep in spite of spending the evening with Jared. Since he wasn't due to bring Caroline home until later, she changed into ragged cut-offs and an old T-shirt at noon, then put her hair up in a ponytail. She would help Mike wash the car.

A while later, on her knees on the wet driveway, she called to Mike, "Toss me that soapy rag. You missed a spot over here."

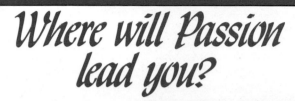

"I never!"

"You most certainly did," Rachel answered, laughing.

Mike dunked the rag into the suds, then, with it still dripping, threw it over the top of the car . . . just as Rachel stood up. It caught her full across the face and clung there.

Rachel screamed behind the rag and got a mouthful of suds. Fumbling, cursing, she finally flung the rag away. *Listen to him over there laughing. I'll murder that kid.*

But before she could even wipe the soap from her eyes, Mike, bellowing with laughter, had rounded the car and turned the spray nozzle directly on her face. "How 'bout a little rinse, Mom?"

Rachel shrieked as the cold spray soaked her face, her hair, and her T-shirt. "Michael Henry Harding!"

Mike laughed.

"I'll get you for this, you maniac. Jared was right. You can't possibly be my son. Gypsies left you on my doorstep."

She put a hand in front of her face to divert the spray and made a grab for the hose. Mike dropped it and ran to the other side of the car, whooping with laughter.

"I didn't mean it, Mom, honest. It—" His own laughter cut off his words. "It was only an accident. Just a little wash and rinse, that's all."

Rachel aimed the nozzle across the hood of the car. "Wash and rinse? I'll show you wash and rinse." She turned the nozzle from spray to jet and let him have it.

"I give! I give! I'm sorry! I'll never do it again!"

"Don't believe him, Mom. He'll be trying to wax you next."

Caroline.

Rachel spun around at the sound of her daughter's voice, jet nozzle still in her hand. The spray caught a laughing Jared square in the face.

Caroline and Deb squealed and ran from the spray bouncing off Jared as he tried to dodge the deluge.

Realizing she still gripped the nozzle, Rachel finally had sense enough to release the handle and cut off the water. She could do no more than gape at her drenched boss, who looked as if he didn't know whether to laugh or strangle her.

"Time to leave," Caroline yelled. She grabbed Deb by the arm and headed for the house.

"I'm with you." Mike followed, hot on their heels.

The slamming of the front door finally penetrated the thick fog in Rachel's brain. Her lips twitched involuntarily. A small sound escaped. Then a louder one. In the next instant she burst out with full-throated, uncontainable laughter.

After a moment of laughing at Jared's sober expression, she tried to turn away from him and accidentally planted one foot squarely in the bucket of soapy water.

That set Jared off, and before long they were somehow clinging to each other, both of them weak with laughter.

Still chuckling several minutes later, Jared lifted her out of the bucket and stood her on the driveway. "Here," he said, bending to pick up the hose. "Let me help."

"Don't you dare!" Rachel, thinking she was going to get soaked all over again, tried to run.

Jared stopped her with a hand around the back of her knee. At the innocent, playful gesture they both stopped laughing. Their eyes caught and clung. Their smiles died. Rachel's breath halted. His touch was like fire. A very pleasant fire. His eyes, too, spoke of heat, and want. As his gaze trailed down her face, her skin tingled, as if he were stroking her.

When his gaze scorched a path to her trembling breasts, she gasped but refused to look down. She hadn't worn a bra. Her shirt was soaking wet. She could feel it clinging to her and knew it was transparent by now. Her nipples, already puckered from the cold water, tightened even more under his hot gaze.

Jared knelt before her on one knee, his hand still holding her leg, his gaze on her quivering breasts plainly visible through the soaked T-shirt. He tried to swallow. Nothing happened. He tried again. His hand around her knee tightened, as did the hand holding the nozzle, in an effort to keep from reaching up and rediscovering the firmness of her flesh.

They were both brought back to the world with a jolt when he squeezed the nozzle too tight, and a frigid spray caught her across the legs and him in the face. He released the nozzle instantly, and closed his eyes and took a deep breath.

"I think I needed that," he murmured.

He squeezed the nozzle again, gently this time, and rinsed the soap from her leg, following the spray with his hand. The sensation of cold water and hot, hard flesh trailing up and down her calf sent rivers of heat circulating through Rachel's body.

Jared cut off the spray, released her leg, and stood up slowly, only inches away. With an index finger he wiped a droplet of water from her cheek.

"I know you," he said softly, his deep voice sending tingles down her spine, his eyes once again holding hers captive. "You're my new friend,

Rachel. We met last night." He brushed another drop from her nose. "Hello, Rachel."

The moisture left her mouth and pooled in other places, secret places, places that shouldn't be moist. Not here. Not now. Not with . . . her boss. A trembling seized her, but it wasn't of fear.

"The . . . ah . . ." She had to stop and clear her throat. "The children are probably watching. Let me go, Jared."

His eyes slowly roamed her face. "I'm not holding you," he whispered.

It was true, she realized with a start. He wasn't touching her. Not physically. She felt foolish then, felt her cheeks heat up. She tore her gaze from his face and walked shakily to the faucet to turn off the water.

Jared followed. "We came early, hoping you and Mike could go to lunch with us. My treat."

How could he sound so calm, so casual, when she was coming apart at the seams? Instead of answering him, she went in the house and to her room, where she dried off and changed clothes, at the same time trying to regain her equilibrium.

Rather than go out, since most of them were still a little damp around the edges, Rachel fixed sandwiches. Jared acted as though nothing had happened, while Rachel played with her food and tried to stay on the opposite side of the room from him.

Yet when he and Deb left an hour later, and Rachel, Caroline, and Mike were playing Scrabble on the living-room floor, Rachel somehow felt . . . robbed. Of her senses, her peace of mind. Of his warmth. His presence.

It didn't help any that Caro kept talking about him. About how nice he was, how good-looking, how much fun.

Rachel found herself listening avidly to a detailed description of every room in Jared's large two-story house, the big-screen TV, the swimming pool in the backyard, and Nora Allred, Jared's gray-haired, widowed, live-in housekeeper, who made her own doughnuts from scratch.

Listening to Caro was one thing. Listening while Mike watched her like a hawk was something else entirely. He was much too observant for her peace of mind.

What did that look on his face mean?

Six

Until she'd run into Jared at the softball game, Rachel had been seriously considering dropping at least part of her disguise. If she had to wear a bra, she'd at least rather wear one the right size.

But after the way Jared reacted to seeing the real her, and equally important, the way she'd reacted to him, she decided firmly against it. The less she revealed of herself, so to speak, around Jared Morgan, the better.

So Monday morning it was the same familiar bag lady who showed up for work. But she could tell by the look in Jared's eyes, after the irritation fled, that her disguise wasn't all that safe anymore. He knew what lay beneath it.

She tried to ignore the feelings—fear, anxiety, and, yes, anticipation—his look stirred. She strove for friendly distance when she passed his desk to get herself a cup of coffee from his kitchen.

When she came back out into his office, her first thought, when she saw his empty chair, was one of relief. He'd left. Then she saw him at the door, closing it, and walking slowly, purposefully, toward her.

She cleared her throat and licked her lips. "Did you want something?"

He gave no answer, just kept coming, he and those damned jungle-cat eyes. And like a jungle cat, he was stalking his prey. And she was it.

Rachel meant to hold her ground, she really did. But her knees began to shake. In an effort to steady them, she took a step back. "What are you doing?"

He just kept coming. When he stood directly in front of her, a deadly serious look on his face, she swallowed heavily. She couldn't take her eyes from his. She felt like a deer caught in the headlights of a car. She couldn't move. Couldn't look away.

"I promised myself," Jared began as he took the coffee cup from her hand and set it on his desk, "that I wasn't going to push you into anything you weren't ready for. I know we agreed to pretend that night in Las Vegas never happened, but I can't do it anymore," he said. "I can't pretend I don't know what your lips taste like against mine, what your hands feel like when you touch me."

"Jared, don't."

"Can we talk about it?"

"There's no point, and you know it."

"Because you're afraid of me?"

It might be simpler letting him think that, but she couldn't let him blame himself. "It's not you I'm afraid of. It never was."

"Maybe, if we took it slower this time . . ."

"It doesn't matter, Jared. Even if I got over my fear, there are too many other reasons you and I should stay just friends."

"Name one."

"For starters, it's a good way to mess up our working relationship."

"I know," he said. "I've never . . . been attracted

to my own secretary. Not to any employee. It goes against my own rules, my own common sense." His gaze roamed her face. "But that doesn't seem to matter to me anymore. I can't get you out of my mind at all. I think I'm going crazy. I've been this way since before Las Vegas."

Rachel was dumbfounded. "Before?"

"Yes, before." He brushed a strand of black hair from her cheek. With a wave at her wig and her clothes, he said, "Why are you still dressing this way? If you want me to back off, just say so. But if you think this costume of yours is going to discourage me, think again, lady. I want you. I think I've made that obvious."

Rachel held his gaze for as long as she could, then looked away. How did she tell him that she wanted him, too, but that she was afraid? Afraid she would panic again in his arms. Afraid if she didn't, she would end up disappointing him. Afraid of what she feared would be only a casual fling to him, of what he'd think of her if he found out about the rest of her past, the part he didn't know yet.

Afraid he'd walk out of her life and she'd never see him again.

The phone in the outer office buzzed. She slumped with relief. *Saved by the bell. How trite, but true.*

"I . . . have to get the phone." She pulled away from him, eager to go yet reluctant to leave. His look said he wanted her to stay. She picked up her coffee, spilled a drop due to her shaking hands, and left the room.

A half hour later she was still shaken by his words but was starting to function normally again. She really had no choice—the damn phone wouldn't quit ringing. The world wouldn't stop so she could get her act together.

The phone rang yet again. This time it was Peter Michaelson, the news director. After hanging up a moment later, she had to force herself to go in and talk to Jared.

"Peter says he'll be up in a few minutes to introduce his new reporter to you."

"Fine." He lowered his head to sip his coffee but didn't take his eyes off her. It made her want to fidget.

"I'll, uh, be in the mail room. I . . . need to use the copy machine."

She managed to stay away from the office for twenty minutes before deciding she'd rather not have Jared come looking for her. Slowly, reluctantly, she headed back down the hall.

As she approached her door, she heard male voices from within Jared's office. Peter came out first and nodded to her. Another man, about five foot eight, red hair and narrow shoulders, wearing a plaid sport coat, had his back to her and was shaking hands with Jared.

"Welcome aboard, Lyle. It's good to have you," Jared said sincerely.

Lyle. No. Her stomach knotted. It couldn't be.

Rachel halted beside her desk, rooted to the spot. Fear and dread poured through her veins.

"Thanks," the smooth reporter's voice answered. "It's good to be here."

The man turned toward her. Rachel gasped and turned her back, clutching frantically at the edge of her desk. The room spun crazily as she tried to think. *Think, dammit.* A second later she remembered she was in disguise. Surely not even Lyle Shotz, ace reporter from St. Louis, Missouri, could recognize her now. After all, it had been a long time. Even if he'd been looking for her, he wasn't looking for a frumpy woman with black hair.

Jared frowned at Rachel's behavior. She'd always been polite and friendly to everyone who'd come to his office. Never had he seen her deliberately turn her back on anyone, much less a new employee. In fact, she was more inclined to go that extra step and show the new person around and make him or her feel welcome.

He glanced at Channel 3's newest reporter to judge his reaction to Rachel's behavior. The man looked at her briefly, then looked away. His eyes seemed to catch at something on her desk. He stared at it for a long moment, then looked sharply back at Rachel, who puttered nervously with the stack of papers in her arms, her back still to him.

When Lyle Shotz ran his gaze slowly, deliberately, down Rachel's back, then up again, Jared stiffened. A wicked gleam sparkled in Shotz's eyes, and a self-satisfied smile parted his lips.

"Well, well," Shotz drawled. "The world just keeps getting smaller and smaller. Hello, Rachel Anne."

Rachel's stomach rolled over and heaved. He recognized her! But how? *Dear God, how?*

This couldn't be happening. She couldn't have come all this way, gone through all this trouble to build a new life for herself and her children, only to have *him* show up and recognize her. It just couldn't happen.

But it had happened . . . was happening. Here and now. What was she going to do?

She turned around slowly.

"I wondered what had happened to you," Shotz said with what to Rachel looked like a particularly vicious gleam in his eyes. "It's good to see you again."

Rachel's skin, from her face to her feet, turned

cold and clammy. She could feel Jared and Peter staring at her, waiting for her to greet their newest employee. For her it would be like welcoming a viper into her nest.

"That's right," Jared said. "Rachel is from St. Louis too. I hadn't thought you two might know each other."

Shotz grinned. "Oh, yeah. We've known each other a long, long time, haven't we, Rachel? Although, I must admit, you do look, ah, different from the last time I saw you."

Knowing she had to answer, Rachel hugged her stack of papers tighter against her chest and swallowed the sour taste in her mouth—the taste of fear and revulsion. She tore her gaze from his eyes and stared at the papers in her arms. Her knees were shaking. She managed a jerky nod and said, "Shotz."

Peter said something then, but all Rachel heard was a buzzing in her ears. She thought Jared answered, then Shotz, but their words were merely sounds battering against the panic that threatened to send her running from the room.

Running. She latched on to the word. Could she run again? Could she pack up her children and leave town?

She wanted to, badly. Her chest swelled with the urge.

But could she? Could she take them out of school for a second time this year and drag them God only knows where? They were just settling in. Running meant uprooting them, forcing them to start over making new friends. Another city, and for her, another job search. Holding her breath and praying no one would recognize her.

Oh, God, what was she going to do?

Her breath rasped in her throat as though she

were already running. Running for her life. The papers in her arms started slipping away. Rachel blinked and found Jared taking them from her. Frantic, she searched the room. Gone. Thank God. Shotz was gone. Peter too.

"Rachel?"

She couldn't look at Jared, at the questions she knew would be in his eyes. Her breath came harder, her heart whacked against her breastbone.

"Rachel, talk to me."

Talk? She wanted to cry, to scream . . . to run. But talk? No. She couldn't. Her vision blurred.

Think. She had to think, to calm down. Decide what to do. Her choices seemed to narrow down to just two. She could do nothing and wait for Shotz to tell what he knew, or she could run.

Oh, God, help me, help me.

Jared took her arm, alarmed at how badly she trembled. Something was drastically wrong, and he intended to find out what. He'd never seen anyone so pale in his life. "Rachel, are you all right?" Stupid question.

She didn't answer, just kept gasping for breath and jerking her gaze around the room, eyes wide and glassy with what he swore was sheer terror. His heart ached for her, even as he wanted to shake her and demand to know what was wrong. In the state she was in, he doubted he would get any answers. She didn't seem to be aware he was even in the room. She didn't seem to be aware of anything.

Whatever was wrong, it obviously had something to do with Shotz, with that part of her past she had never revealed. She was terrified.

Past. Terror. Jared's chest tightened. Could Shotz be the one who had attacked her? Cold rage filled him.

His rage, and his questions, would have to wait. If he didn't get Rachel to calm down and breathe, she would hyperventilate and pass out.

"Rachel, it's all right." He led her slowly into his office and closed the door behind them. "It's all right, it's just you and me. Take it easy."

She wasn't hearing him. Her mind was still on whatever had set her off. And she was breathing harder, getting paler by the minute.

His own hands were none too steady when he pulled her into his arms and felt her violent trembling. Her chest heaved hard and fast. The wheezing sound of her breath made his throat ache. "Ah, damn, Rachel."

He ran a hand up her back, trying to soothe her, and felt where the damn bra that squashed her chest flat cut into her flesh. No wonder she couldn't breathe.

He reached beneath her jacket and tugged the back of her shirttail free from her skirt. The bra was so tight, he couldn't release the clasp. "Hang on, honey, hang on," he murmured. "We'll get you some air in just a second." He tried again and heard something rip as the clasp came free. He felt her lungs expand.

"Okay. It's okay now."

He held her gently in his arms, terrified of scaring her even worse, yet unable to let her go. With his hand still beneath her blouse, he stroked her back and encouraged her to breathe slowly. "Easy, sweetheart, easy. That's it. Just breathe."

Jared blinked sudden moisture from his eyes. She was hurting so badly. *What?* he wanted to ask. What had happened? What threat did Shotz pose?

As he slowly stroked the bare skin of her back, unbidden tendrils of heat curled through his veins. He cursed himself for wanting her at a time like this.

But then, it seemed he always wanted her. Every minute of every day. Even right now, when she was so upset. Right here in his office, with a hundred people milling around less than twenty feet away.

He squeezed his eyes shut and wrapped his arms loosely around her.

Rachel's breathing finally slowed. She stirred in his arms, then shivered. Still holding her close, he led her to the sofa across from his desk. Carefully, gently, as if she were made of fragile glass, Jared sat her down.

When Rachel became aware of her surroundings, she was surprised to find herself on Jared's couch, with his arm around her. His strength and warmth felt so good, she leaned against him and sighed.

An instant later it all came rushing back.

Lyle Shotz was here. Her past had just caught up with her.

She tried to straighten, but Jared held her close. "It's all right, it's only me. Rest a minute and catch your breath."

Her breath? There was nothing wrong with her breath. Then she remembered that terrible feeling of suffocating, of not being able to draw air into her lungs. She took a cautious breath, then another, savoring the simple act of breathing.

"I'm all right now." She pulled away, and this time he let her go.

"Is he the one?" Jared asked slowly. "Is Lyle Shotz the man who attacked you?"

Rachel blinked. Considering the way she'd panicked, she could see why Jared would ask that. "No." She shook her head.

"Then do you want to tell me what happened just now?"

What could she say? He'd taken care of her, helped her when she needed him. All she wanted to do was fall into his arms again and stay there, safe and warm forever. Instead, she was going to lie to him. "I'm not sure. Maybe it was something I ate."

Jared took her hand and held it firmly. When he spoke, his voice was soft, yet it held a ring of steel. "Look at me, Rachel."

"Jared, please." She tried to pull her hand from his suddenly tight grasp.

"Look at me, damn you."

Rachel swallowed the bile that rose to her throat and turned her eyes to face his hard, uncompromising gaze.

"It was not something you ate."

Each word came out sharp, determined. Certain. She tried to look away, but his eyes wouldn't let her.

"We've been together nearly every day for three months now. We've shared good times, bad times, and a lot of in-between times. I'm attracted to you, you know that. I care about you, and I think you feel the same. So what in the hell does it take to get you to trust me?"

Rachel stared into his bright green eyes, reading anger, even pain, in their depths. She should tell him. She should just tell him and get it over with. She no longer believed he would react the way others had. She should just say it. Simple. No problem.

"Jared, I . . . I . . ." She closed her eyes so she

wouldn't have to look at him and tried again. "I . . . oh, damn. I . . . I can't."

"Can't what?" he demanded harshly. Then his voice softened as he released her hand and stroked a knuckle across her cheek. "Can't trust me enough to tell me what's wrong?"

She opened her eyes and felt the sting of tears. "It isn't that," she said, shaking her head. "Not really. I just . . . can't talk about it. Not right now."

She pulled away from him then and was grateful that he released her. His touch was too compelling.

She rose and was halfway to the door before she realized why she felt so comfortable. Her bra was unfastened. She stopped and folded her arms across her chest before turning around and heading for his bathroom. "Excuse me."

In the bathroom Rachel forgot what she'd been about to do and sagged against the wall.

Shotz. Lyle Shotz was here. What was she going to do?

She closed her eyes and tried to think, to plan. There seemed no other way except to tell Jared the truth, yet she had tried a few minutes earlier and hadn't been able to.

What was she going to do?

"Rachel?" Jared called from outside the door. "You all right in there?"

Rachel took a deep breath and straightened away from the wall. "I'm fine," she called. "I'll be out in a minute."

Remembering why she'd come to the bathroom, she reached beneath her blouse and found one side of her bra clasp ripped from the fabric. It was ruined. After undressing enough to take off her bra, she put her blouse and jacket back on.

She started to toss the bra into the wastebasket,

but, no, the basket was empty. She didn't want Jared or the janitor to see her underwear, for heaven's sake. She tucked the bra into her jacket pocket.

She straightened her wig, took another deep breath, then left the bathroom. Jared stood beside his desk. "Anything wrong?"

Only everything, she thought. Then she frowned at him. "You ruined my bra."

He raised a brow. "Good. I'll ruin the next one, too, if you ever try to stuff that thirty-four-C body of yours into a thirty-two-A bra. You damn near passed out earlier because you couldn't breathe. It's stupid, it's dangerous, it's got to be uncomfortable as hell, and it isn't necessary. If you'll recall, I've already seen the shape of what you're trying to hide."

He came closer. "And while we're on the subject," he said, taking a menacing step in her direction, "get rid of that damn wig too. Whatever you're hiding from, my guess is that it just caught up with you. If it isn't just your modeling, and if he's not the man who attacked you, then what's going on? Talk to me, Rachel."

She wanted to, knew she should. "I . . . I can't. I'm sorry. Not just now." She left him there and returned to her desk.

The events of the morning put Rachel behind in her work. A half hour past quitting time she was still there. Unfortunately, so was Jared. She had the sinking feeling he intended to stay as long as she did, whether he needed to or not.

When she walked past the door to his office on her way to get a soft drink, she kept her gaze averted.

Expecting the cafeteria to be empty, Rachel was panic-stricken to find Lyle Shotz heating a sandwich in the microwave.

Shotz ran his gaze casually from her head to her toes and back again. "I'll say it again, Rachel Anne, you sure do look different from the last time I saw you."

White-hot anger settled like a glowing ember in the pit of her stomach and fought with the terror already there. "Still invading people's privacy, Shotz?" When he only smiled at her, she asked, "Just out of curiosity, how did you recognize me this morning?"

"You've got to be kidding." His smile widened to show a set of perfect white teeth. She wondered why he didn't file them. Surely, they should be more pointed. "With all the footage I've got of you, do you honestly think I could ever fail to recognize those legs? Besides," he added with a cocky grin, "I recognized your maiden name on your nameplate."

Rachel turned her back on him and jammed her money into the coin slot of the soft-drink machine, then whopped the third button with the side of her fist.

"Since we're going to be working together, maybe you'll finally give me that interview I've been wanting."

"What?" she shrieked, spinning around to gape at him. "After the stories you did about me in St. Louis? You've got to be just about the cockiest bastard that ever walked. Don't you even *think* about doing another story on me, or I'll—"

"You'll what? I'd be careful with threats if I were you," he said, his smile never slipping. "The way I figure it, the only reason for a woman to disguise her looks to the extent you have is that you don't want someone to know who you are. Like maybe our esteemed boss? Would I be messing up your little setup here if I happened to whisper a few tidbits in his ear?"

Rachel's body went from boiling hot to freezing cold in an instant. "You're just cruel enough to do it, aren't you?" she whispered.

"What's happening here?"

Rachel stiffened at the sound of Jared's voice.

"I could hear the two of you all the way down the hall. Would either one of you like to tell me what the hell is going on?"

Between the reporter's arrogant threats and Jared's obvious anger, Rachel felt trapped. She had to get out of there. Now! Let Shotz tell his dirty little tales. What did it matter? She couldn't stop him anyway. Men like Shotz had no conscience, no finer side to appeal to.

It was over. All her plans, her hopes for a stable future for herself and her children, her dreams of living peacefully, anonymously. Over.

She pushed her way past Jared and ran down the hall toward her office. She cut the corner too sharply and caught the drinking fountain with her left hip. Her breath sounded harsh to her ears, and she had to double over and clutch her side while trying to run the rest of the way to her desk.

With tears clouding her vision, she picked up the phone. Her hands shook so badly, she had to start over three times before she punched in the right numbers. When she started to give the address for the taxi, Jared caught her by the shoulder and took the phone from her hand.

In a grim voice he said, "I'll drive you home."

He didn't say a word during the entire trip. His silence made Rachel want to scream. Everything made Rachel want to scream.

When he stopped the car and killed the engine, Rachel had her door open before she realized they weren't at her house. Instead of turning on her street, he had driven another block and parked the car at the far end of the supermarket parking lot. "What are we doing here?"

He took a deep breath, then let it out. "You need a little more time before I take you home." At her inquiring look, he said, "If you walk in your door looking like you do right now, your kids are going to think you've had a run-in with an ax murderer. Just sit here a minute. Let a little color come back to your cheeks."

Rachel pulled her door closed and slumped back in the seat. He was right. She even felt pale. She must look like the walking dead. "Thank you," she whispered.

After a few minutes Jared leaned toward her and braced his arm on the seat back behind her head. "Rachel, talk to me. You're important to me. Tell me what's wrong."

Rachel stared at him in dismay. *Important?* "You don't even know me."

"Then tell me. Tell me who you are. Tell me whatever it is that's so terrible it makes you react the way you did today. There's nothing you could say that would change the way I feel about you."

Rachel pressed her fingers to her throbbing temples and gazed, unseeing, out the window at the traffic on the street. It was all she could do to keep from wailing.

She cleared her throat. "Shotz can tell you plenty, if you really want to know."

"Dammit, I don't want to hear what he has to say. I want to hear it from you, whatever it is."

She dropped her hands and clenched them until her nails dug painfully into her palms. "I can't,

Jared, I just can't. But if you meant what you said . . . if . . . if I mean anything to you, then don't listen to him. Don't talk to him." She swallowed and forced her hands to relax. "It doesn't matter anyway. There's nothing for you and me. Nothing. It's pointless."

Jared felt as if he'd been punched in the gut. Nothing for them? Pointless? No. Never. He couldn't, wouldn't accept that. He took her face in both hands. "Is this pointless?" He brushed his lips against hers and felt the spark he'd known would come. He tasted, nibbled, then kissed her fully. When she whimpered, he started to pull back, afraid he was scaring her. But her lips clung to his, and Jared knew he was lost.

He groaned, wanting to wrap his arms around her, wanting to crush her close against his chest. Close to him, flush against him, part of him, where she belonged. He clamped down on the urge, afraid of pushing her too far, too fast.

His heart thundered. Ragged breathing filled the car. Jared felt his control slipping away and tore his mouth from hers before it was too late. He leaned his forehead against hers and gasped, "Not pointless. Not pointless, Rachel."

When his breathing finally slowed, he started the car and drove her home. She didn't say a word before getting out and walking to her door.

Jared returned to his office and let out a weary sigh. When he sat down and rubbed at the ache in his neck, he noticed someone had left a three-quarter-inch videocassette on his desk. Beneath the logo of a St. Louis TV station were scrawled the words "Rachel Anne." He picked it up, frowning, wondering where it had come from.

The answer came immediately. *Shotz.*

Whatever was between Shotz and Rachel, the man obviously knew her secrets. Secrets she had not confided in Jared.

He reached for the tape, then drew his hand back. He wanted to know her. Wanted to know all about her, backward and forward, inside and out. Everything about her. But dammit, he wanted her to *tell* him her secrets. He didn't want to find out from some impersonal videotape someone had sneaked into his office.

In seconds he was at the small wet bar pouring himself a tall glass of straight Jack Daniel's. His hand shook so badly, the neck of the bottle clattered against the rim of the glass. When he tried to take a drink, bourbon sloshed out and ran down his hand.

He couldn't stop himself. He picked up the cassette and slammed it into the tape machine behind his desk. After a few seconds of color bars, a slate popped up on the screen:

Shotz   November 3
Length: 5:07 Rachel Anne/background

The slate stayed on-screen for half a minute, followed by black. Jared's hand trembled. He had three, maybe four, seconds before the video would start. That little time to change his mind.

Seven

With a vicious oath Jared rammed his fist against the "eject" button. The machine whined; the tape slid out. Jared stared at it and took a gulp of his drink. Jack Daniel's seared all the way down to his stomach, where it caught fire and made him shudder.

Watching the tape, to him, would be an invasion of Rachel's privacy. Never mind that half of St. Louis had probably seen what was on there. He would feel like a Peeping Tom. He didn't want to see some reporter's version of her life. He wanted her to tell him.

With careful, deliberate movements, Jared pulled the tape free of the machine and set it on the far corner of his credenza, with the label facing the wall.

Then, with shaking hands, he poured the rest of his drink down the drain and walked out of his office.

Jared overslept the next morning. The price one paid for spending the night with Jack Daniel's. Jared had come home from the office and gone straight to the wet bar in his den. Damn. He wasn't used to this. He couldn't remember the last time he'd had a hangover.

When he got to the station, a half hour late, there was a note on his desk saying Rachel had called in sick. He started to phone her but didn't. He dropped his briefcase on the desk and walked out.

Her car wasn't home, but then Mike probably had it at school. She didn't answer the doorbell.

"Rachel, open up. I know you're in there."

Nothing. She didn't answer. He pounded on the door. Not until he threatened to beat it down did she finally open it.

"I thought I better check on you." He brushed past her and entered the house. "You're not sick, are you?"

Rachel clasped her arms around her stomach and turned away from his penetrating gaze.

"You're still upset over that argument you had with Shotz last night."

Rachel's heart fluttered in her chest. Slowly, she turned to face him. "Did you talk to him?" she asked, her voice breathless, her nerves in shreds.

"Shotz?" He hesitated only briefly, then said, "No, I didn't talk to him."

Rachel nearly collapsed with relief. She'd been granted a reprieve. It was temporary, she knew, but she'd take it.

When Jared placed his hands on her shoulders, warmth and life flowed into her. "Come here," he whispered. Then his arms closed around her and pulled her against the hard wall of his chest, and it was like nothing she'd ever known before. It was shelter and safety; it was warmth and comfort. It was like coming home.

When his lips nuzzled her temple, she nuzzled

back. He trailed kisses across her fluttering eye-lids, down her cheek, until he captured her mouth in a kiss so tender, she wanted to cry. It seemed forever, yet only a second, before he pulled away and looked into her eyes.

Again she wanted to cry, at the tenderness and caution she saw in those dark-green depths. He kissed her forehead, then cradled her head against his shoulder.

"I swear, Rachel," he said in a voice rough with emotion, "I'll try my hardest not to rush you into anything you're not ready for. I won't pressure you into telling me what's wrong. But I'm not about to let go of you, lady. Not now, not ever. I can't."

But he did let her go a moment later, and left to return to work. Rachel stared out the living-room window at the driveway and watched him leave. She hugged her arms around herself, try-ing to recapture the warmth and security of his embrace. It didn't work.

A bright blue sky and the new green of spring didn't go with her heavy thoughts. Jared's vow of holding on to her forever should have reassured her. Instead, it terrified her. If he knew the truth, would he change his mind? She turned from the window.

She was falling in love with a man. Her head snapped up, and her heartbeat quickened. She *was* in love with him! It was so simple. Why hadn't she realized it before?

She knew the answer to that one though. She didn't want to love a man. Love meant being hon-est. It meant trusting another person. She wasn't sure she was ready to do either.

But whatever happened, she knew she couldn't hide out at home. With determined strides she went to the bedroom and searched for something to wear to work. She was through with the tight bra and sloppy clothes, and good riddance.

As far as her relationship with Jared went, the wig might as well stay home too. But how would she explain the long blond hair to the others at work? Her new figure was going to be enough of a shock.

One step at a time, girl, she told herself. That's how she would handle her job, her coworkers, Lyle Shotz, and Jared. One step at a time.

When the taxi let her out at the station an hour later, Jared was plainly surprised to see her.

"I thought you were staying home today."

Rachel stared at him through the door to his office. "I, uh, changed my mind."

Something flickered across his eyes, too fast for her to interpret. A corner of his mouth almost curved up. "Was it something I said?"

She hesitated, then her mouth twitched in answer to his. "Maybe."

His eyes roamed intimately over her figure, noting the real shape of her. He smiled. "It's good to have you . . ."—his gaze settled on her wig—" . . . almost back."

She gave a jerky nod and turned toward her desk, flustered as usual with his close perusal. Flustered, but flattered. And excited. And scared.

More than a few people during the day commented on her "new shape" and "new clothes," not the least of whom was Mike when he picked her up from work.

A slow grin spread across his face when she climbed into the car. "Nice to have the old Mom . . . almost back." His eyes flicked to her wig as he spoke.

Rachel laughed. "Jared said the exact same thing."

Mike centered his gaze on the road and pulled out of the parking lot. "He did?"

"Well, he didn't call me Mom."

Mike drove in silence for several minutes, a thoughtful look on his face. "He still doesn't know about you-know-what?"

"No," she answered with a sigh, her light mood evaporating.

"Somebody's bound to recognize you and remember. What happens then? You know he's gonna find out. Think he'll give you a bad time?"

Rachel had never tried to hide anything from her children. Except—she hadn't told them what actually happened in Las Vegas. She'd only said he'd seen her. Close enough.

She would have shielded them from the ordeal five years ago if she had been able, but Mike and Caro had been caught in the middle. Even if they hadn't been, the media coverage of the whole ugly story had been too widespread. Mike had even caught some of the boys at school talking about her.

So she didn't try to hide anything from him now. "I meant to tell you last night, but I . . . well, I couldn't."

"Tell me what?"

"We hired a new reporter yesterday. Lyle Shotz."

"Goddamn."

"Michael!"

"Sorry. He didn't recognize you, did he?"

"He did. He guessed why I was disguised and threatened to tell Jared everything if I don't give him an interview."

Mike chewed on his bottom lip. "What are you gonna do?"

Rachel dropped her head against the seat back and closed her eyes. "I don't know. I'm not giving him an interview, that's for sure."

"Think he'll really tell the coach?"

"I wouldn't put anything past that buzzard."

"What if he does tell him?"

What if he does? Rachel had been asking herself that one over and over. She still wasn't sure of the answer. "Jared won't react the way others have. But I don't really know just how he will react. I imagine he'll think what most everyone else thinks—that I . . . well, you know. I don't think he'd fire me, unless the station ended up getting some bad publicity over the whole mess."

"But you're worried about what he's gonna think of you when he finds out, right?"

She swallowed past the lump in her throat and blinked the sudden fog from her eyes. "When did you grow up on me, Mike? How did you get to be so smart?"

Mike's knuckles whitened as he gripped the steering wheel. "I grew up on the sidewalk in front of the county courthouse in St. Louis, when I was twelve years old."

She could see him trying to force himself to relax, and she hurt for him. He was her son. She was supposed to be able to shield her children from pain, but life didn't really work that way. Not for her. Not for her children.

To have their own father walk out of their lives when they'd needed him the most had been a crushing blow. For Hank to have totally ignored them, with the occasional exception of an impersonal child-support check during the past five years, was unforgivable.

"As for being so smart," Mike said a moment

later, a grin curving his lips, "I take after my old lady."

"Hey. Watch that 'old lady' stuff, will ya, kid? I'm feeling every one of my years today."

"Oh, I don't think you have anything to worry about."

"And how's that?"

"I don't know what your boss thinks of you, but I'd say the way a certain softball coach looks at you, you've got a few more good years left."

"Michael!" Rachel felt her cheeks heat up. A nervous laugh escaped her lips. "You're imagining things."

"No," he said, a thoughtful frown wrinkling his brow. "No, I'm not. I think he means it, Mom. I think he really likes you. The Bluejays have lots of mothers and older sisters hanging around at practice and the games. He's never looked at any of them the way he looked at you the other night. And he sure never left the park with any of them before."

When Rachel didn't say anything, just stared out the side window and played with the clasp on her purse, Mike prodded. "Well, do you like him or not?"

She ignored the dull ache of hopelessness and managed a smile for her son. "Yes. I like him. I like him a lot."

A moment later he said, "Well?"

"Well what?"

"So what are you gonna do about it? You just gonna sit around and wait for Shotz to tell his version of what happened?"

"Meaning I should tell Jared myself," she said, not expecting an answer. "I know I should. But it's going to take me a while to work up to it."

When they pulled up into the driveway at home,

Mike grinned at her. "So, when does the wig go?"

"That's something else it's going to take me a while to work up to," she said with a laugh. "I haven't figured out quite how to explain it to everyone at work."

That night, in keeping with her "honesty-at-home" policy, Rachel sat Caroline down and told her what was going on.

Caro surprised her with, "Well, I don't think you have anything to worry about. Coach is the neatest, nicest man I've ever known. And he likes you, I can tell. And, Mom, he's *so* good-looking," she added, rolling her eyes to the ceiling dramatically. "Don't you just *drool* every time you look at him?"

Rachel laughed. "Not quite, sweetie." *It's more like I melt.*

"And just think," Caro went on, her twelve-year-old imagination soaring. "If you and Jared got married, Deb and I'd be sisters."

"Now hold on," Rachel cried, shocked. "Mike asked if I liked him, and I said yes. Nobody said anything about anything else."

"Yeah, but, Mom—"

"No 'but, Mom.' " She had to squelch Caro's outrageous idea immediately. Jared might care about her, but what would happen when he learned the truth? She didn't want her children hurt any more than they already had been.

Damn you, Carl Sutton. Five years later, and you're still ruining our lives.

"This conversation does not leave this room," Rachel said firmly. "Do you understand? I won't have you thinking thoughts like that. I've been single for a long time, and so has Jared. I don't think either one of us is too willing to change that, especially since we're just friends."

If you and Jared got married . . .

Caroline's words wouldn't leave Rachel alone. And that was absurd. It would never happen. She didn't want it to happen. The very idea terrified her.

She pressed the print command key on her computer and waited for the laser printer to spit out the letter she'd just typed. She wanted to put it on Jared's desk before he arrived. When the sheet emerged, she picked it up, then stood and turned around.

And ran smack into Jared.

A small cry escaped her. The letter crumpled between their bodies.

Jared put his hands on her shoulders and grinned. "Heck of a good morning." Then the teasing glint left his eyes, replaced by a heart-stopping mixture of tenderness and fire. Her lips parted.

"If you don't stop looking at me like that," he said, "I'm liable to embarrass both of us, here and now, in front of whoever happens to walk by."

But Rachel couldn't look away from his eyes. Heat spiraled through her body. Her feet refused to move. Her eyes refused to lower. She felt her heart pound against his.

"Rachel," he whispered hoarsely. His hand came up toward her face.

Rachel gasped and spun away from him. She managed to walk around her desk and sit down. She barely made it before her knees gave way.

Jared placed both hands on the front edge of her desk and leaned toward her. "Have dinner with me tonight."

His voice, low and husky, sent shivers down her spine. She could almost feel his arms around her, his lips brushing hers, even though he was no longer touching her. "I, uh, don't think that's . . . a good idea."

"Oh," he said smoothly, "I think it's an excellent idea."

"Please, I mean, thank you, but . . . no."

He looked at her for a long minute, then straightened. "All right. I said I wouldn't push." He thrust his hands into his pants pockets. "You coming to the game tomorrow night?"

"Yes." She breathed a sigh of relief when he moved away. His nearness was overpowering.

Rachel somehow made it through the rest of the day. It helped that Jared refrained from any more personal comments. He left her pretty much alone, except for a certain look now and then.

The next day was a bit easier. There was a lot of work to be done, and in spite of the tension, she had to admit they did work well together.

It also helped that he left work early to run some errands before the Bluejays game that evening.

Even though Mike had to drop Caro off at the field, then get Rachel and take her home to change clothes, they still made it to the field before the game started.

It came as a complete surprise to Rachel to see Cynthia Morgan in the stands. Jared hadn't mentioned his mother was in town.

"Rachel, how good to see you again," Cynthia cried.

The woman seemed genuinely delighted to see her, but Rachel's heart pounded as she sat beside

Jared's mother. Rachel hadn't spoken to Cynthia since that day in the Las Vegas conference room, when Cynthia had seen her disguise. What must the woman think of her? What had Jared told her?

What had Cynthia told him? Did she remember the stories? The publicity that had spread nation-wide? Had she told Jared?

Of course she remembered, Rachel told herself. It had been there in Cynthia's eyes when they met in the restaurant. But she obviously hadn't said much to Jared, because he still didn't know the truth. If he did—

Rachel forced the thought away and greeted Cynthia, then introduced Mike to her.

"Jared didn't mention you were in town." Rachel regretted the words as soon as they left her mouth. Of course he hadn't mentioned it. It was none of her business. Yet she'd made it sound as though she had a right to know.

Cynthia didn't seem to think the question out of place at all. "He was afraid if you knew I was here, you wouldn't come to the game. He thought you might not want to see me after we bumped into each other when I came to get him for lunch that day."

Well, the woman certainly believed in having things out in the open. Rachel bit back a grimace. There was no getting around Cynthia Morgan. "I, uh, was more than a little embarrassed to have you see me like that."

"It's quite all right," Cynthia said with a smile. "When Jared explained about the trouble you'd had with other jobs, I understood perfectly. Oh!" She suddenly looked startled, then glanced at Mike, then back at Rachel.

Rachel smiled. "It's all right. Mike and Caro

both know about it." Her smile died then. "But I'm afraid Jared doesn't. Not really."

"I take it you're referring to certain highly publicized parts of your past? You haven't told him?"

Rachel glanced away and shook her head.

"Well," Cynthia said, "that's your business, not mine. But if you trust him enough to let him see you like this," she said, waving a hand at Rachel's long blond hair and tight blue jeans, "to know who you are, I don't really see why you don't trust him with the rest."

When Rachel didn't answer, just squirmed in her seat, Cynthia spoke again. "You're afraid of what he'll think of you if he knows?"

Rachel kept her eyes on the toes of her shoes and nodded.

"Do you really think a man like my son is so shallow?"

Startled, Rachel straightened and looked directly at Cynthia. "No. I don't think he's shallow at all," she declared. "It's just—"

"Never mind, dear," Cynthia said, patting Rachel's tight fist. "You'll work it out somehow. Like I said, it's none of my business anyway. Oh, look. The game's starting."

Rachel had been so intent on her conversation with Cynthia that she hadn't paid attention to anything else. When she looked up now, Jared was striding toward them, a grin on his face.

"Well," Cynthia demanded, "is our team going to win?"

Jared ignored her question. He ignored everyone and everything as his eyes centered on Rachel's, capturing her gaze. Without looking away, he asked, "Mike, how do you feel about men making passes at your mother?"

Rachel gasped.

Cynthia sputtered into silence.

Mike, startled at first, allowed a deep chuckle to escape. "Well, now, Coach. That depends on whether or not my mother likes it."

Jared's grin widened as his eyes traveled to Rachel's trembling lips and back. "Oh, she'll like it," he drawled, stepping up into the bleachers. "I promise."

He grasped Rachel's face in both hands and planted a swift, hot kiss on her parted lips. Startled blue eyes stared into laughing green ones. Jared tore his mouth away. "For luck," he whispered over the laughter and catcalls going on around them.

Jared turned his back and walked away. Rachel felt like hiding beneath the bleachers. Good Lord! Had the man lost his mind? She glanced around and realized that nearly everyone in the stands and on the field had seen that kiss. She turned beet red, clear down to her toes.

Out on the field Caro and Deb exchanged secret smiles. Next to Rachel, Mike laughed at the look on her face.

"Personally," he said, "I think you should go for it, Mom."

"Go for it?" Cynthia's mouth twitched. "My, what an appropriate phrase."

If possible, Rachel blushed even harder.

The Bluejays took the White Sox, 10–6. Jared insisted that the Morgans and the Fredrick-Hardings celebrate the win at a nearby Mexican restaurant. The girls chose to ride in the Mustang with Mike and Rachel, since the top was down.

They all met in the center of a crowded parking lot that separated the casual Mexican restaurant from an elegant steak house. The night air was warm with the promise of summer soon to come, and the two families laughingly followed the aroma of refried beans and chili through the parking lot.

At the door to the restaurant Jared maneuvered so he and Rachel were the last to enter. No one noticed when he took her hand in his and squeezed.

He didn't take his gaze off her all through dinner. He watched the way her eyes lit up when she looked at her children. He watched the way she got along so well with Deb and his mother. He watched the way she licked the spicy hot sauce from her lips.

He felt like groaning. Or better yet, grabbing her. That kiss at the ballpark had done absolutely nothing to cool the raging heat that roared through his blood.

She needed him. In her life, and in her heart, she needed him. She needed his arms around her. She needed to be able to lean on someone—on him—now and then. She needed him to make her laugh.

All he needed was for her to admit it.

Two days later, Cynthia was back home in Denver, Jared was back in Las Vegas for the National Association of Broadcasters convention, and Rachel was alone in the office.

She'd been racking her brain for a way to explain her way out of the blasted black wig. The thing was driving her crazy, and there really wasn't a need for it anymore. She still expected Shotz to spill his guts any day now. Why bother with the uncomfortable wig?

While eating lunch in the coffee shop with a group of employees, she listened to several women talking about new hairstyles. She took a deep breath and plunged in.

"Speaking of hairstyles, I'd better warn you, none of you will even recognize me tomorrow."

"You getting a perm or something?" Cathy from accounting asked.

"Not exactly." Rachel grinned. "This," she said, tugging on her hair, "is a wig. Tomorrow I won't be wearing it."

"That's a wig?"

"It looks so natural."

"So what are you going to look like?"

"When I took this job," she explained, "I had a lot of bills to pay. I've finally got them taken care of, so tonight I'm getting my roots done. My hair's pretty long, and I keep it, or rather I *try* to keep it, blond. Thought I'd better warn you. I don't want anybody barring the door on me in the morning."

There, she thought as the conversation around her resumed. *That should do it.* Chances were almost nonexistent that any of them would ever learn she was a natural blond.

"Won't Jared be surprised when he gets back," someone commented.

Yes. Won't he.

And he was. Friday morning when he walked into the office, he stopped at her desk to say hello. Instead of speaking, he simply stared.

There she sat, in clothes that accented her figure, her long blond hair streaming, curling down her back and across one shoulder, a tentative smile on her face. His hands ached to bury themselves in her hair.

"Welcome back," Rachel whispered, her throat suddenly gone dry.

His smile started in his eyes and was bright enough to light the world. "Thank you. It's good to be back. You have no idea how good." His eyes searched her face for a moment, then settled on her hair again. "I don't think I've ever been greeted by anything more beautiful in my life."

Her smile widened a fraction. "Coffee's ready. How was the convention?"

"Long," he said without moving. His smile died slowly. "And lonely."

Rachel lowered her eyes. "You know you're making me uncomfortable, don't you?"

"Sorry," he said, taking a deep breath. "Coffee, right?"

"Right. Coffee."

Saturday evening, after another Bluejays victory, Jared should have been jubilant, and he was until he looked up from loading equipment into the trunk of his car to see Rachel's—or was it Mike's?—red Mustang pulling out onto the street.

Damn. He hadn't even had a chance to talk to her. But then, she'd probably planned it that way. The lady was definitely skittish.

"Need a hand, Coach?"

Jared looked up, surprised to see Mike standing beside him. "What are you doing here? I thought I just saw your car leave."

"That was Mom. I'm going home with Freddy Howard for the night. Well, I see you've already loaded everything. See ya later."

Now that was sure interesting. Mike had known Jared was finished loading, so why had he come over and volunteered that tidbit of information? What difference could it possibly make to Jared if Mike Harding spent the night with one of his friends? And more important, why did Mike want him to know?

A moment later realization dawned on him, slow but sure. *Well, I'll be damned.* He'd almost forgotten. This was the night Susan Thompson, his left fielder, was having a slumber party for the whole team. All the girls would be there. Right this minute, Mr. and Mrs. Thompson were herding a giggling, screaming gaggle of twelve-year-old girls into their big van.

Deb was going. She'd brought her clothes and sleeping bag with her. Just then she ran up and gave him a quick hug.

"See ya tomorrow, Dad," she called as she ran toward the overflowing van.

And Caroline Harding was right behind her.

Well, I'll be damned.

Anticipation lit a fire in his chest as he hurried home to shower and change. "Need any help, Coach?" Jared muttered to himself with a laugh. "Yes, and thank you, Mike Harding."

Rachel sat on the couch and listened to the silence echoing all around her. It was rare for her to be home alone. It was eerie. It was lonely.

Then, into the roaring quiet, other sounds intruded. City sounds of movement, of life. Heavy Saturday night traffic on Northwest Sixty-third behind her back fence. A siren off in the distance somewhere, probably headed for Baptist Hospital, or Deaconess. Hard-rock music blared from a car radio going past her house, followed a few minutes later by another car, this one blasting country and western.

A car door slammed nearby. Her doorbell rang. When it rang a second time, Rachel jumped with surprise, only then realizing it was indeed her doorbell.

She knew who it was without answering, but she answered it anyway. When she flipped on the porch light and opened the door, there stood Jared, a scowl on his face.

"Don't you even look out the window before you open the door when you're home alone at night? I could have been the neighborhood strangler."

Rachel held the screen door open with a laugh. "Neighborhood strangler? You've been watching too much television."

"In our business, I'll have you know, there is no such thing as too much television."

When she closed the door, quiet descended again. Only this time it was different. It was a Jared quiet. It throbbed and pulsed vibrantly, expectantly. She throbbed and pulsed with it.

He'd obviously been home since he left the ball-park. His clothes were clean and fresh, dress slacks and a short-sleeved pullover. No trace of the dust and sweat that had coated him earlier.

"I would have called first, but I was afraid you'd tell me not to come."

Rachel was stunned to read hesitancy in those brilliant green eyes. His very uncertainty put her at ease. She tilted her head and gave him a slight, curious smile. "Why did you come?"

"I wanted to see you. To be able to look my fill, maybe even reach out and touch you once in a while without starting an avalanche of gossip. To talk to you." He smiled again then. "To listen to your voice say something other than 'You have a phone call.' "

They both laughed at that, then stopped laughing when Jared reached out and stroked her lips with his finger. His voice grew husky. "Maybe even to kiss you again, this time without an audience."

When his lips lowered to hers, she couldn't have moved away if she'd wanted to. And she most certainly did not want to. What started as light and tender, a mere touching of lips, quickly turned into something much more potent when his arms came around her and crushed her to his chest. Panic was the furthest thing from her mind.

Rachel's hands, with no help from her head, slid up his arms and around his neck. Her fingers thrust themselves into his soft dark hair. Her lips clung to his. Her heart beat rapidly against his. Her thighs brushed his.

And when he moaned, she moaned.

His hands spread fire across her back. His tongue stroked hers, in and out, matching the rhythm of his rocking hips as one hand lowered to her hips and pressed her firmly against the hard proof of his desire.

Jared tore his mouth away and gasped for breath. He rested his chin on top of her head, and gradually, finally, their breathing slowed.

"I'm sorry," he said softly. "I meant to keep it light and easy."

Rachel was nearly devastated by the storm of emotions his kiss unleashed in her. She wanted to laugh. She wanted to cry. She wanted to shout to the world, "This gorgeous, beautiful, wonderful man wants me, and I didn't panic in his arms."

And at the same time she wanted to run and hide, to cover up her past, to shield herself from possible hurt.

What am I going to do?

Suddenly, Jared chuckled and kissed the top of her head. "How did you ever get to be a fashion model, anyway? I thought all models were tall and skinny." His hands ran up her ribs and brushed the sides of her breasts, taking her breath away. "And flat-chested," he added, laughter still in his voice.

Rachel shuddered at the feel of his hands. "I was an icebreaker."

"Don't I know that. You broke my ice a long time ago, lady."

He moved to kiss her again, but this time Rachel forced herself to turn away. "Please don't, Jared."

"Why?" The laughter was gone, replaced by a ragged huskiness. "You didn't get scared this time." She tried to pull free of his arms, but he held her tight. There was no panic in her eyes. "Something happens when we're together, something special. I know you feel it, too, so why do you keep pushing me away?"

She went limp in his arms, her hands resting on his shoulders. "I don't push you away nearly as often as I should," she said. "And every time I don't, I feel like I'm leading you on. This . . . thing between us, whatever it is, is very likely leading nowhere. It just . . . complicates everything."

"I'm sorry it's so complicated for you." Jared raised her face and forced her to look at him. "For me it's very simple. I want you." He brushed her lips with his. "I'll take as much or as little as you're willing to give. I want it all, but I'll take what you'll let me. And I don't just want to take, Rachel. I want to give too."

Rachel searched his eyes for a long moment, reading his sincerity, forced to believe him.

He placed a quick kiss on her nose and released her. "Enough serious talk. Do you have anything to drink? All this kissing makes me thirsty."

Rachel stepped back and shook her head. Should

she laugh or scream? The man was driving her absolutely crazy. And by the look on his face, he knew exactly what he was doing to her.

"We have a variety of soft drinks, plus milk, pineapple juice, orange juice, and apple juice. Take your pick."

Jared raised a brow. "You always keep such a large selection on hand?"

She laughed and headed toward the kitchen. "I don't have a choice. We each like a different kind of juice and a different brand of soft drink."

"Who am I stealing from if I have orange juice?"

"That's Mike's."

"Your son has impeccable taste."

"He'll be glad to hear it."

"Well, it's true." Jared grinned at her. "He even likes me. Shows how smart he is."

Rachel narrowed her eyes in a mock glare. "What makes you think he likes you?"

"Well," he drawled, "I figure if he didn't like me so much, he wouldn't have made it a point to let me know you were home alone tonight."

"He what?" This time her glare was for real.

"Now don't get excited. He knows I'm trust-worthy."

"Ha. 'Said the spider to the fly.' Wait till I get my hands on that little traitor. Somewhere in his upbringing, I must have made a wrong turn."

Jared took the can of juice from her and grasped her hand. "You don't really mind that he told me, do you? That I came over?"

Rachel glanced down at their joined hands, then back up at his face. "No," she whispered, sudden-ly feeling shy. "I don't mind."

"Then would you do something for me?"

"What?"

"Kiss me."

Rachel felt her heart skip a beat. "But we just—"

"No, that was me kissing you. I want you to kiss me."

She swallowed and moistened her lips, but she didn't move toward him.

"Please."

Rachel's knees nearly buckled. Was she supposed to be able to resist the plea in his eyes and on his lips? The plea in her own heart? She hoped not, because if so, she was going to fail.

Heart pounding, hands shaking, she stepped closer and raised her head. He met her gaze but not her lips.

So he wasn't going to help. But Rachel didn't care, for she suddenly wanted to kiss him more than she wanted to breathe. Boldly, she put her hands behind his head and pulled his mouth down to meet hers.

At the first touch of her soft lips on his, Jared's breath caught. The orange juice can gave slightly beneath the pressure of his fingers as he struggled to keep from wrapping his arms around her. This was her kiss. He wanted her to do it her way.

Her tongue brushed his lips. He shivered and opened his mouth to hers. The sweet, gentle kiss turned hot. Her hands clutched his head tightly. He moaned.

"Kiss me back, Jared," she whispered. "Put your arms around me and kiss me back."

With another moan, this one of surrender, Jared dropped the juice can to the floor and complied. He had thought to make her want him so much, she would forget whatever fear might be hovering in her mind. His plan backfired. It was he who forgot her fear as he wrapped his arms around her and pulled her against him.

He forgot everything but Rachel. She was like liquid fire in his arms, in his blood. She fit against him as though made for that express purpose. And when she moved against him, a pulse pounded strong and steady in his loins, dragging him deeper into the kiss.

Rachel reveled in his response. Breathless, eager for more, she pressed herself against him. Fire and yearning engulfed her. With her hands on his back she imagined what his skin would feel like, hot and sleek to her touch. She imagined what his weight would feel like pressing her down against her mattress, his legs tangled with hers. She felt his hardness against her and imagined him filling the aching emptiness deep inside her.

And then she imagined she heard Hank's voice. *. . . disappointing, at best.*

Jared felt the change in her instantly. This was different from the panic that had gripped her that first time they'd kissed. Rather than struggling, she went still. And cold.

"What is it?" he whispered.

She shook her head. "I'm sorry. I guess I'm just not ready for this."

"Could have fooled me," he managed.

She pulled back and looked at him. "I didn't mean to."

He'd pushed too hard again, dammit. He gave her a slight smile. "I know you didn't. I didn't mean to let things get so out of hand either. I just can't seem to help it. You take my breath away."

She swallowed. "You . . . do the same to me."

His smile came slow and sure. "Good." He kissed her again, tasted her soft, alluring sweetness, then let go. "I think I've pushed my luck far enough for one night."

Eight

During the next few weeks, as school let out and summer rolled in, Rachel hardly ever thought about the secret she was keeping from Jared. When thoughts of it did intrude, she shoved them aside. Later. There would be plenty of time for explanations later.

Even Shotz seemed to have backed off. She'd only seen him once in the past several weeks. He'd been coming out of the newsroom, and she had been heading toward him on her way to the coffee shop. When he spotted her, he did an abrupt about-face and ducked back through the door.

Well, she thought with a satisfied smile. *Maybe the man has a conscience after all.* He'd made no attempt to talk to her since their confrontation weeks ago, when Jared had walked in on them.

And Jared had been as good as his word. He wasn't trying to rush her into a more intimate relationship. But he wasn't backing off any either. Every day was a test of her willpower to resist the heated suggestions in his eyes and the lingering touches when no one was looking. And every day her willpower slipped another notch.

He was definitely getting to her. She wanted

him. She could freely admit that now, at least to herself.

Physically wasn't the only way she wanted him, however.

They could laugh with each other now, as well as work. When they disagreed on something, there was no pouting or petty insults or anger. There was only simple argument. They got along so well, despite the mounting sexual tension that practically sizzled around them, that Rachel began to long for more than just physical things.

She wanted to lean on him and cry on his shoulder when Mike left home in a year or two. She wanted to sit beside him and watch as their daughters became women. She wanted to let him catch her beneath the mistletoe at Christmas, when her hair was gray and her skin wrinkled. She wanted to watch his face light with joy when their grandchildren came to visit.

Grandchildren? Good grief, Rachel.

She shook her thoughts away with a frown and poked a pencil into the electric pencil sharpener on her desk. At least Jared had kept his promise not to rush her. In fact, he'd been "not rushing" her so much, they hadn't even been alone together since that night Caro and Mike had both been gone. The night of the slumber party. The night she had lain awake after Jared left and wondered if maybe, just maybe, if they made love, he wouldn't think she was a disappointment.

There was another Bluejays slumber party planned for Saturday night after the game, but she and Jared certainly wouldn't be getting together during this one. Deb was hosting it. Jared Morgan's home was about to be invaded by twelve-year-old girls.

Jared walked in just then and caught her laughing. "What's so funny?"

"I was just wondering how you're going to survive tomorrow night's invasion. Think you can handle it?"

"My dear madam," he said. "You are looking at a veteran of several such invasions, I'll have you know."

"Oh, well, pardon me," she said, trying to achieve a straight face and failing. "I should have known."

"Actually," he said, "Nora's handling the kitchen, and I'm the combination outdoor chef and lifeguard. I could possibly use a little help in that area," he added, looking up at the ceiling thoughtfully. Then he narrowed his eyes. "Any volunteers?"

"What?" she said, feigning shock. "You mean you're actually admitting you might need help?"

They bantered back and forth for several minutes, then Jared stopped laughing and said, "How about it? Will you come? If you'll help me keep an eye on them in the pool, after I throw them out, we could swim for a while. You wouldn't really have to do any work."

Rachel accepted without hesitation. After all, it wasn't as if they'd be alone. How out of hand could things get with an entire softball team to chaperon them?

Rachel spent half of Saturday trying on swimsuits she hadn't worn in years, trying to decide on one. Maybe she should buy a new one? She was tempted to do just that until she ran across the maillot she'd bought in Acapulco one year. It stretched over her body like a second skin, swirling from turquoise to royal blue to navy to black, and was cut high at the hips. Tiny straps draped her shoulders, then crisscrossed down her back to tie near the base of her spine.

A bikini would be more revealing, and for that reason she chose the maillot. Her bikinis barely covered the essentials, and made no attempt at all to cover anything else. Lord! She'd actually worn those things in public.

She chose a black, loose-weave cover-up that had short sleeves and ended at midthigh. Suit and cover-up were so flimsy, they both rolled up and fit into her purse with hardly a bulge.

One adult volunteer and a dozen screaming Bluejays bouncing off the walls over their unbroken winning streak descended on Jared Morgan's single-parent household that night.

How all twelve girls managed to cram themselves into Deb's room and change into their swimsuits while there was beyond Rachel.

Nora, Jared's middle-aged, matronly housekeeper, showed Rachel to an upstairs guest room, one of several, so Rachel could change clothes. She put on the suit, cover-up, and sandals, then studied herself in the full-length mirror on the closet door.

Her face and arms were tanned just from going to the softball games. But her legs were pale. No help for it.

She'd expected to be nervous about this evening, but, oddly enough, she wasn't. She looked forward to spending time away from work with Jared, yet not alone with him.

Although she had to admit she did want to be alone with him. Every day she fell a little further under his spell. Every day, under Jared's warmth, Hank's vicious taunt lost a little more power.

Where it was all leading, she didn't know. She only knew Jared made her feel alive, for the first time in years. He made her want things she thought she'd never want again, and he filled her with promise that he would fill those wants. All she had to do was let him. And she was tempted. Oh, so tempted.

But not here, and not tonight. Tonight was for the girls. For fun.

Rachel followed the sounds of giggles and girl-talk down the stairs, through a comfortable-looking den, and out the sliding glass doors to the patio and pool.

Hickory smoke drifted on the light summer breeze. She turned to find its source and found more. Jared stood at the grill, spatula in hand, his eyes moving deliberately over every square inch of her.

She returned his perusal and felt a fluttering in her chest. He wore nothing but revealing black swim trunks. It was only the second time she'd seen him other than fully clothed, and the sight of all that sleek tanned skin stretched taut over the curves and dips of his muscles took her breath away. Her fingers tingled, wanted to thread themselves through the dark furring on his chest.

Finally, their eyes met, and Rachel found herself standing directly before him, having no idea how she got there.

"Hello," they said in unison. Then they smiled at each other.

Jared tore his gaze away and cleared his throat. He turned two hamburger patties on the grill before looking back at her. "I thought you and I could eat while the girls swim. Once they eat, they're out of the pool for the night."

"Where's Nora?" asked Rachel, glancing around.

Jared chuckled. "She's in the kitchen making the rest of the patties."

"I should probably go help her."

As she stepped away, he grasped her arm, smiling. "No way, lady. You agreed to help me, not my housekeeper. You wouldn't really leave me alone with all these girls, would you?"

A few minutes later they sat at a glass-topped wicker table near the grill, out of normal splashing range, and kept an eye on the swimmers while they ate and tried to talk over the shrieking and laughing of young girls and the blare of rock music blasting from a portable tape deck.

Jared's eyes kept skimming down, trying to see through the loose weave of Rachel's cover-up.

Two other sets of eyes, youthful and mischievous, were also looking at that cover-up. "We've got to do something," one girl whispered.

"Yeah," the other answered. "If we don't, she'll wear that thing all night."

Around sundown the Bluejays decided they were ready to eat. Jared and Rachel covered the grill with hamburger patties and lined the table with paper plates, mustard, catsup, mayonnaise, sliced cheese, sliced pickles, sliced tomatoes, shredded lettuce, three kinds of chips, and four kinds of dip. An ice chest next to the table overflowed with soft drinks.

When all the meat was cooked, Jared flipped on the pool and yard lights, then led Rachel to the other end of the patio, where they stretched out side by side on matching chaise longues.

A few girls sat on lawn chairs, but most simply sat on towels spread out on the hot concrete.

"Hey, Dad!" Deb hollered. "We need more chips."

When Jared didn't move, Rachel started to get up.

"Sit still," he warned. "They'll have us waiting on them hand and foot all night." To Deb he called, "There's more in the kitchen. Ask Nora."

"I thought I came here to help," Rachel said.

"You did. But if you're determined to indulge someone's every whim, indulge mine." He threaded his fingers through hers and brought their joined hands to his chest. "The girls can take care of themselves."

"Jared." She tugged to free her hand, even though she wanted to hold on. "Let go. The girls are watching."

He looked across the corner of the pool and met several direct stares, two in particular more intent than the others. Deb and Caro were grinning from ear to ear.

"Let them," he said with a shrug. "I don't think the sight of a man and woman holding hands will do any irreparable harm."

When she refused to relax, he released her hand. She glanced back at the girls. Deb and Caro were frowning.

Soon the girls got up and started tossing empty paper plates into the trash can and headed indoors, taking their music with them. There was a moment of silence, then a different tune blasted the air when Deb turned on MTV.

Through the sliding glass doors, Rachel and Jared watched the girls shove aside coffee tables, chairs, and footstools so they could dance.

Surprisingly, Deb and Caro came back outside to help their parents clean up.

"You girls go on back in," Jared said. "We can handle this."

"That's okay, Dad. We want to help."

Jared shrugged at the two earnest faces. "Suit yourselves."

When everything was neat and orderly, Caro picked up the last remaining open jar of mustard and started past Rachel. In a neatly executed maneuver, Caro managed to trip and fall against her mother. Rachel staggered back, then caught Caro by the shoulders.

"Oh, Mom, look what I've done," Caro wailed dramatically.

Rachel followed her daughter's gaze and sighed as a large glob of mustard slid down the front of her cover-up, dribbled onto her knee, then splattered between her toes.

"Oh, Mom. I'm sorry. Here," said Caro, yanking black buttons through crocheted loops. "I'll go rinse it out before it stains. And I'll clean your sandals too."

Rachel tried to back away from the eager fingers, but Deb came to help. "Really, girls, it's—" Too late. Cover-up and sandals were stripped from her in seconds. "Uh, thank you."

"Don't mention it," said Deb, backing away. "I mean, it's the least we could do, right, Caro?"

"Right. Oh, Deb! Look out!"

Deb spun around and tripped. She put her hands out, caught her balance for a moment, then stumbled into Jared. His cry of surprise was cut off the instant he hit the water and went under.

When he came up sputtering for air, Rachel stood at the edge of the pool laughing, the two girls behind her.

"Oh, you think that's funny, do you?" he growled. He glanced past Rachel, then grinned at her.

Behind her she heard a giggle. Hands thrust against her back. She sailed through the air to land with a big splash, right square in Jared's arms. Her shriek ended in a gurgle.

She came up shouting, "Caroline Marie!"

"You're too late," Jared said between bursts of laughter.

Rachel pushed away from his chest, shaken by the feel of his wet, slippery skin, and turned toward the house while treading water. The girls could at least have pushed them into the shallow end!

She was just in time to see the two culprits step through the sliding doors. One of them said something about Cupid. A duet of giggles floated back, then the glass doors slid shut, followed immediately by heavy, lined drapes swishing closed.

Behind her Jared was still laughing.

" 'Oh, Mom, look what I've done,' " she mimicked. "I'll murder the little devil."

"No, you won't," said Jared, still laughing. "You've got to admit, the whole thing was pretty clever on their part."

Rachel chuckled, then sucked in her breath when his warm hands slid around her waist from behind and pulled her back against his chest. Hot lips nuzzled behind her ear as hair-roughened thighs slid against hers beneath the water.

She gasped. "Jared."

"Lord, but you feel good," he whispered, trailing his lips down her neck. "I've been wanting to put my arms around you, feel you next to me, all night."

His lips, his hands and legs, and the warm, sensuous feel of the water, robbed Rachel of all thought, except one: She wanted more. "Oh, Jared," she moaned.

An instant later the pool and patio lights went out, leaving Rachel and Jared with nothing more than starshine and the glow from the nearby windows. Jared threw back his head and laughed.

"Those little devils," Rachel muttered.

"Relax." His deep voice rumbled in his chest and vibrated right through Rachel's back, sending shivers down her spine.

"Cold?" he asked, wrapping his arms more tightly around her.

"No," she whispered. "I think our daughters have gone a little overboard."

"You heard them," he answered. "They're playing Cupid." He turned her around in his arms and nipped at her cheek. "It would be a shame to let all their efforts go to waste."

His lips were warm, his tongue was hot, and Rachel was lost. He leaned back into the water and took her with him, drifting toward the shallow end. When his feet hit bottom, he lifted her in his arms. Without breaking the heated kiss, he located the steps and climbed from the pool into the warm night air.

At a darkened upstairs window a curtain moved aside. "Did it work?" whispered Deb, struggling for a place at the window.

"Did it ever!"

"Wow!"

"Let's get outta here before somebody finds us."

"Yeah, right."

The curtain fell back in place.

At poolside Jared allowed Rachel's legs to drift to the ground. When she stood, she leaned into him, and he groaned. The kiss deepened, became fierce, desperate.

"God," he gasped, tearing his mouth away. "I can't stand much more, Rachel. It's all I can do to keep from taking you here and now, witnesses be damned."

The pictures his words conjured behind her closed lids made Rachel moan. "What are you trying to do to me?"

One hand roamed over her back while the other cradled her head against his shoulder. "I guess I'm trying to make you need me, want me, the way I need and want you. And I don't mean just physically—you know that, don't you? I want that, too, but I want more, Rachel. So much more."

"Oh, Jared. I—"

"Ssh. It's all right." Her heart pounded against his chest. Damn. He was rushing her. If he wasn't careful, he'd scare her away entirely. "You don't have to say anything."

"But I do." She raised her head, searching his face in the dim light from the window. It was time, Rachel knew. Time to stop letting Hank ruin her life any more than he already had. There were still parts of her past she might never be able to leave behind, but those were things she couldn't control. All she could control was her own reaction to what had happened. It was time to let at least part of it go.

She traced a trembling finger across Jared's lips. "I want you."

For an instant, just for an instant, Jared froze. Then his eyes lit and his arms crushed the breath from her lungs as he hugged her. He scattered hot, fervent kisses across her cheeks and nose. "My God," he whispered with a shudder. "You don't know how long I've waited to hear you say those words."

She admitted it. He couldn't believe she finally admitted it. She wanted him! But he wanted more from her. When was she going to admit she loved him?

If possible, the kiss they shared then was even

more desperate, more passionate, than the one before. Rachel couldn't hold her feelings in any longer. Tears seeped from beneath her lashes and ran down to their joined lips.

Jared drank them in, then sipped a salty trail up each cheek.

"I want you," she whispered shakily.

"Rachel, Rachel," he said, somewhere between a laugh and a groan. "Don't say it again. Not now, please." In spite of his words he held on to her, pulling her tight against him.

Rachel moaned. "The girls."

"Yes, the girls."

"They're only a few feet away."

"I know."

"We're supposed to be chaperoning them."

"I know."

"I'm sorry." She nuzzled her nose into the damp hair on his chest. "I wasn't thinking."

Neither was he, really. If he had been, he would never have kissed her. Whenever he kissed her, he ran the risk of losing control. What he wanted from Rachel at that moment was inappropriate, at best, with a houseful of young girls to chaperon. Still, he couldn't seem to stop. He kept trailing kisses down her neck and across her shoulder, taking a thin black strap with him on his way.

"Jared." She gasped. "Jared, we can't."

His shoulders stiffened beneath her hands. Slowly, he pulled the strap back over her shoulder. "You're right."

For long minutes they held each other tightly, waiting for the passionate storm to ease. It took a while for breathing to calm and heartbeats to slow.

When they went into the house, they used a different door than the girls had. Neither Jared nor

Rachel was ready to face a room full of inquisitive eyes. In the upstairs hall he held her close and whispered suggestively, "Hey, lady, you need any help getting dressed?"

She answered with a throaty chuckle, the tension draining away, but not the awareness, or the excitement. "Not if I really plan on getting dressed."

He heaved a dramatic sigh and let his arms slip away. "True. Too true."

They met in the hall again a few minutes later, dressed but with hair still damp. He draped his arm around her shoulders and hugged her close against his side. "I wish you didn't have to go," he whispered, looking deeply into her bright blue eyes.

"You understand why I have to, don't you?"

"Of course I do. I even agree it's best. But that doesn't mean I have to like it."

The closer they got to the den, the louder the music. They stopped in the doorway, and Deb and Caro danced their way over to say good night to Rachel. A few other girls who noticed them waved.

"What time should I pick you up tomorrow?" Rachel asked her daughter.

"No need," Jared said hastily. "I'm driving several other girls home, and I have to take the van back to Susan's parents. I can save Caro for last. When I drop her off, maybe we could all have lunch. My treat."

Rachel watched the secret look of satisfaction the two girls traded. "If you'd wrap her feet in concrete and drop her off in the middle of Lake Hefner, I'll treat us to lunch."

"Mother!" cried Caro, feigning shock. "What a terrible thing to do to your own daughter."

"I must have gotten it from you," Rachel said,

tweaking Caro's nose. " 'Night, girls. Have fun, but don't tear the house down."

" 'Night, Mom. See ya tomorrow."

" 'Night, Mrs. Fredrick."

Then a loud whisper, as Jared led Rachel toward the front door. "Did you see? Did you see the way he had his arm around her?"

"Ssh! You want them to hear?"

A round of girlish giggles followed.

Jared kissed Rachel good night at the door, a kiss so full of tenderness and longing, she nearly wept again.

She drove home in a daze, a silly grin parting her lips.

If the next week at work hadn't been so busy, Rachel was sure she'd never have lived through it.

The 10:30 P.M. movie, which Jared was calling *The Early Late Show,* started airing Monday night. The rating period, that event that comes four times a year to television, when audience numbers are estimated—supposedly scientifically—for each program, started Wednesday.

Thursday, Jared paced the floor, waiting for the unofficial overnight ratings to be phoned in. He had a good feeling about the movie, but he was still anxious. If it went well, other stations in the corporation might follow his lead. If it went poorly, it would be a long time before he'd be able to try that type of program change again.

Rachel jumped every time the phone rang, as anxious as Jared to know how the movie was being accepted by Oklahoma City viewers.

Finally, he stood before her desk and said, "I can't take any more of this. I'll be in engineering. The only call I want to know about is the Call."

Rachel put her hand on his and offered him a smile. "It'll work, Jared. I know it will."

He stared at her a moment, then closed the door to the hall. He walked around her desk, lifted her by her arms, and planted a quick, fierce kiss on her surprised lips. "I love you, Rachel Fredrick."

He let go of her, and she fell back onto her chair. In seconds he had the hall door open again and was headed out.

Rachel sat there, stunned, staring after him. He didn't mean it, she told herself. Not really. He was just glad for her support. She forced herself to breathe normally, told her heart to quit pounding. Jared Morgan was not in love with her. It was just a convenient expression he'd used.

And that was the simple truth.

She wished desperately he hadn't even said it.

A half hour later the call they'd been waiting for finally came. Rachel watched nervously while Jared listened and jotted down numbers. When he hung up, he stared hard at the notepad in front of him.

"Jared?"

He raised his head, and a slow, wide grin lit his face. "It's better than I'd dared hope for."

Rachel returned his grin.

The sales and promotion departments held impromptu celebrations when they heard the overnights. A few minutes later Jared located Rachel back in the film department.

"Rachel, I need to see you a minute, please," Jared said.

"Of course." She followed his brisk footsteps down the hall and into her office, then into his, where he shut the door. "Jared, what is it?"

"I've just had some more good news," he said, eyeing her in such a way that she wondered if *she'd* think it was good news. "There's another Bluejays slumber party planned for Saturday night. At the pitcher's house."

It didn't take a genius to realize what he was saying. They could be alone. Just the two of them. All night. For a moment Rachel felt panic rising up to cut off her breath. It was one thing to fall prey to his passionate kisses and indulge in pleasure on the spur of the moment. It was quite another to actually plan an assignation.

She'd never done anything like that before, except maybe with Hank, when they'd first been married. But she and Jared weren't married. And he was asking her to make plans so they could be together, alone, intimately.

She looked into those bright green eyes, eyes filled with tenderness. Right then she stopped fooling herself. This was Jared. The man she loved. He might have been joking when he'd said he loved her, but she knew with certainty she loved him.

She smiled then. "Your place or mine, mister?"

Jared let out his breath and hugged her tight. "I don't care. Whatever you want."

I want you, she cried silently. Then she forced herself to focus on more practical matters. If she went to his house, the kids wouldn't know where to reach her if there was an emergency. If he came to her house and spent the night, his car would be in her driveway the next morning, bold as all get-out for the neighbors to see.

So be it. Her children's safety came first. "Mine then. I'll fix us a late dinner after the game."

"What about Mike?"

"He's staying with Freddy again. It's already planned."

"Bless that boy," he said fervently.

* * *

By the time Rachel got home from the game Saturday—another Bluejays victory—she was a nervous wreck. Jared would be there in an hour and a half.

What was she going to wear? How should she act? She was definitely apprehensive about the evening, but she wanted this night with him, wanted it desperately.

But she felt so damned dishonest, not telling him about her past. She'd have to tell him, she knew. If she ever hoped to build a solid relationship with him—and she did hope—she had to be honest with him. Somehow, some way, she had to find the courage to tell him the truth.

A cold chill of foreboding washed down her spine. He would find out. One way or another, he would learn the truth. She just had to make sure he heard it from her first. As if that would make any difference.

But not tonight. Tonight was hers.

When he arrived, right on time, she was warmed by the look of appreciation in his eyes. She wore a royal-blue silk caftan that belted at her waist in front and bloused loose in the back. Dainty gold sandals and bare toes peeked out from beneath the hem when she walked.

"You look . . . sensational," he breathed.

She thanked him, suddenly shy at the hot, avid look in his eyes and all that it implied. His look of knowing promise reminded her just exactly what would happen here tonight. They were going to make love. She knew it; he knew it.

They were going to make small talk over a glass of the wine Jared had brought with him. Then they would have a nice civilized dinner and more

small talk. Afterward, she would lead him to her
bed, where they would—

Oh! Her shyness was burned away to cinders as
heat and desire flamed through her. If anticipation could kill, she'd be terminal before the wine
was poured.

She made it through the meal in a daze, her
passion held tightly in check but threatening to
burst forth and consume her at any moment.

Ignoring her protests, Jared helped clear the
table and clean up the kitchen. Then he poured
them each another glass of wine and pulled her
down next to him on the living-room sofa. She
sat stiffly at his side, her hands shaking from just
being so close to him.

His voice came softly, hesitantly, from only
inches away. "Do you want me to leave?"

"What?" she gasped, jerking her head around
to look at him. "No!" She searched his face and
found it unreadable. "What makes you think
that?"

"You haven't said more than a dozen words
to me all evening. You're obviously uncomfortable with this whole situation. If you want me
to leave—"

"Jared, no. I don't want you to leave. It's
just . . . I guess I'm just . . . a little . . . nervous,
that's all."

His expression softened immediately. "Me too."

"You are?"

"Did you think I wouldn't be?"

She tried to smile. "I guess I did."

"Why are you nervous?"

She shrugged and stared at a tiny spot of light
on the lip of his wineglass. "I've . . . never done
this sort of thing before. I'm not quite sure what
to do, how to act."

"Never done what sort of thing?" he asked softly.

Rachel stood and stepped away. "Had an affair."

"Is that what we're having? An affair?"

She tried to laugh, but it came out more like a croak. "Unless I've totally misread what's been happening between us, I think we're about to." She looked at him over her shoulder, her breath caught in her chest. "Aren't we?"

He started to answer, then something changed in his eyes. "What do you mean, you've never had an affair?"

Rachel felt herself blushing. "A little old-fashioned of me, isn't it?"

"How long have you been divorced?"

She sighed. "Five years."

Jared set his empty wineglass on the coffee table. "Not that it's any of my business, but surely in five years there's been a man or two in your life."

She did laugh then, nervously. "I don't know quite how to break it to you, but you're only the second man I've even *kissed* since I was seventeen."

A dozen questions ran through Jared's mind. The least appropriate one came out. "Is it because you were attacked?"

She stiffened.

"I'm sorry. My timing stinks. I shouldn't have brought it up."

"No," she said. "It's all right. I mean, that's not why I haven't . . . there just hasn't been anyone, until you."

Jared rose and stood behind her, not touching her but close enough for his breath to fan the hair at her temple. "Does that mean you don't want me to leave?"

"No. I don't want you to leave. But . . ."

"But what?"

She pressed her fingers to her forehead to still the sudden throbbing. Her harsh bark of laughter came out more like a sob. "It sounds ridiculous, after being married all those years and having two children, but I'm not really . . . very . . . experienced."

Warm, strong hands tenderly cupped her shoulders. She jerked in surprise. He pressed his chest against her back, and she nearly moaned aloud.

"Do you honestly think I care, Rachel? Do you think you'll disappoint me? Is that it?"

She trembled against him. "It's been known to happen."

Jared stilled. "What are you talking about?"

Rachel swallowed. "My . . . my husband, Hank." She swallowed again, trying to ease a path for the words. If she couldn't yet be honest with Jared about everything, she at least had to tell him this. Had to give him the chance to change his mind. "Hank said—"

"Hank was a damned fool," Jared said with a growl. "You couldn't disappoint me in a million years. I want more than just to take pleasure from you. I want to give it. I want to give you more pleasure than you've ever known. But you're not the only one with insecurities. I might disappoint you, you know."

Rachel turned slowly beneath his hands, her heart soaring at his words. She cupped his face in her palms. "The only way you could disappoint me is by leaving."

"Rachel," he groaned. His arms came around her in a crushing embrace. His hands stroked feverishly up and down her back, separated from her tingling flesh by soft, warm silk.

"I'm not going anywhere. I'll never leave you."

Rachel gazed into his fiery green eyes. "Love me, Jared. Just love me."

He moaned, clutching her even tighter. "I do. You know I do. And I will." His hands roamed her body, touching her everywhere through the silk. He groaned again. "Have you got anything at all on under this thing?"

Feeling her mood lighten, she chuckled and buried her face at the curve of his shoulder. "Not much."

He kissed her then, for the first time that night. Tender at first, then hard, hot, demanding. He consumed her, heart and soul, with his lips. His body trembled against hers, and her spirit soared.

By the time they came up for air, they were both trembling. She smiled and took his hand in hers. "Come," she whispered. She led him down the hall to her bedroom, her steps quickening along with her heartbeat. At the flip of a switch a dim golden glow lit the room.

Jared's breath caught in his throat at the sight of the sheets turned down so invitingly on the bed. He squeezed her hand and searched her eyes. "Still nervous?" His voice was husky with emotion.

"Only a little."

He took her in his arms, tenderly, lovingly, and whispered, "Don't be. We'll be good together. So damn good."

His words and the promise in his eyes unleashed a flood of emotion from her heart. Oh, how she loved him. With her hands around his neck, she pulled his head down until their lips met.

He took over all her senses then, and she ceased

to think. All she could do was feel. She felt the heat of his lips, and the tug on the tie at her waist. Strong, tender hands brushed the caftan from her shoulders. It fell to the floor, leaving her standing before him wearing nothing but a thin strip of ivory lace at her hips.

When he stood back to look at her, she went weak from the flame in his eyes.

"God, you're beautiful," he whispered. "More beautiful than anything I ever imagined."

With a hand behind her knees he lifted her in his arms and carried her to the waiting bed. He sat next to her, leaning over her, and ran the tip of one finger from the hollow of her throat to the edge of the ivory lace. Her breath turned ragged at the simple, provocative touch.

She opened her arms to him, wanting, needing his weight pressed against her, and he came to her. His sweater was soft and prickly against her breasts. She squirmed, trying to get her hands beneath the fabric so she could push it away. She wanted his skin. Had to have it beneath her fingers, covering her breasts, surrounding her.

Jared pulled from her arms, and she whimpered at the loss of his warmth. In seconds he was back, gloriously, totally bare, stripping off her tiny swatch of ivory lace. When their bodies met, chest to chest, belly to belly, thigh to thigh, they both gasped.

It was heaven. Somehow, sometime in her life, she must have done something right to be allowed to feel his flesh against hers. To feel the hardness of his desire pressed against her hip. To feel his lips burning a path down her throat to the tip of her breast.

His tongue flicked out to tease, and she sucked in her breath. His lips closed over a nipple.

When he sucked, he magically tugged on invisible strings that ran from the taut peak to down between her legs.

"Yes," she murmured. "Oh, Jared."

He left a trail of fire from one nipple to the other, turning her into a mindless, quivering mass of sensations. She buried her fingers in his hair, moaning almost continuously now, unable to stop the movement of her hips.

Jared's hand trembled on its way to that triangle of pale gold curls between her legs. He had to fight for every ounce of control, because her response, as it had always done, was driving him over the edge.

His fingers delved gently into the secret folds of her flesh, searching, finding the entrance he craved. *Oh, God, oh, God.* She was so hot and moist and ready.

When she cried out his name and thrust her hips against his hand, it was all he could take. He slipped his hand away.

She moaned in frustration and tossed her head from side to side. "No," she cried. "No. Don't leave me."

"Ssh. I'm right here."

He kissed his way from her stomach to her lips, sliding his thighs between hers. He braced himself on his elbows while his hardness sought entrance to her softness. Her hips raised toward him.

"I'm right here," he murmured.

Then he slid into her, slowly, slowly, holding his breath, stealing hers. Slowly. Slowly. Until he was firmly planted. It was heaven. She was everything he had imagined, and more.

He had every intention of being as gentle with her as possible. But Rachel had other ideas. She clutched his hips and rotated hers, and he was lost. They moved together then, faster and faster, to that secret rhythm that comes from within. Faster and faster, until—

"Jar-ed!"

Her nails dug into his flesh at the same time that he threw back his head for one final, earth-shattering thrust.

He collapsed on top of her, trying to keep some of his weight on his elbows. It was several long minutes before either could draw a halfway-calm breath. Jared rubbed his cheek against hers, still stunned by what had just happened between them. Then he stiffened. Her cheek was wet. Too wet.

"Rachel?" He pulled back to look at her in the dim glow of the bedside lamp. Her eyes were dark liquid pools, with tears streaming from the corners. "Did I hurt you?"

"No," she croaked. She shook her head from side to side and wrapped her arms tightly around his back. A deep sob racked her body. "No, you didn't hurt me." After another sob, she pressed her face against his neck. "I'm sorry. I don't know why I'm crying. You didn't hurt me. You didn't. I think I'm just a little . . . overwhelmed."

Jared held her close and eased them over onto their sides, still face-to-face, bodies still joined. Relieved laughter rumbled in his chest. "Only a little?" he teased.

Her husky laugh echoed his. "You're not getting another word out of me."

He cupped her face and wiped the tears away with shaking fingers. The laughter faded from his eyes, replaced by a look of wonder. "You're not the only one who's overwhelmed. I thought I knew it all, had felt all there was to feel, until tonight. Rachel, I've never experienced anything like what we just shared. Never, in my entire life. Nothing has ever felt so right as this, here, now, with you." His lips grazed hers. "I love you, Rachel Fredrick. I love you."

From his voice, his eyes, there was no way she could doubt he meant it. Tears threatened again. All her fear of disappointing him disappeared. She would have answered, except she couldn't for the huge lump in her throat. Then his lips were on hers again, and he moved within her, stoking the fires that had not totally cooled.

Sometime during the night they fell asleep in each other's arms, only to wake and love again. And again.

He stayed until dawn. He would have stayed longer, but they both knew he couldn't be there in her bed when her children came home.

After he was gone, Rachel crawled back into the rumpled bed and sighed a long, contented sigh. She hadn't known it was possible for a woman to be so happy.

Then a shadow crossed her heart. She was going to have to tell him, and soon.

Nine

Rachel didn't sleep after Jared left. She lay on her back and stared at the flecks of light cast on the ceiling by the rising sun. How was she going to tell him? What was she going to say? And how was he going to react? She rolled to her side, frustration, doubts, and fear eating at her insides.

When she finally got up, she was worn out from loving and worrying, and she was no closer to a solution to her dilemma. The only thing she knew was, she had to tell Jared. She couldn't put it off any longer.

And if her worst fears were confirmed—if he wanted nothing more to do with her—well, she'd had one night with him. A night she could treasure for the rest of her life.

But dammit, she was only thirty-five years old. She didn't want to spend the rest of her life with nothing more to treasure than one night in the arms of the man she loved. She wanted more nights with him. And days. And years.

But that was wanting. A dream. The reality was her past. A past Jared might very well not want to deal with. And she wouldn't be able to blame him. A bitter taste formed in her mouth.

When she got to work Monday, she didn't know whether to scream with frustration or weep with relief. She'd made up her mind to tell him. She was going to march right into his office, close the door, and tell him—straight out.

But he wasn't in. The note he'd left her said he wouldn't be in until after lunch. She checked his calendar and realized he had meetings and appointments scheduled back to back all afternoon, and even more meetings tomorrow. For what she had to tell him, she needed more than three minutes between appointments. Monday passed with no opportunity.

When the phone rang at home that night, she wasn't all that relieved that it was Jared.

"I missed you today," he said softly when she answered.

"You were rather busy."

"Yeah, and tomorrow looks just as bad. I have to leave the office around three for a meeting across town. Will I see you at the softball game at seven?"

She bit back a sigh of frustration. "I'll be there."

"Is everything all right?"

"Of—" Her voice cracked. "Of course. Everything's fine."

"Good. I can't wait until tomorrow night. Till then."

"G-Good night."

Only it wasn't a good night. Not for Rachel. Once again she lay awake, tossing and turning, tying the covers in knots around her legs, trying to plan what to say tomorrow.

"You'll never guess what happened to me five years ago."

No. Stupid. He already knew part of it.

Jared, please love me. Please believe it wasn't

my fault. It was an accident. Don't stop loving me. Please.

At work the next morning Jared took one look at the dark circles beneath her eyes and made the movie salesman from MGM wait in the lobby.

It was all Rachel could do to keep from flinching when Jared grabbed her chin and forced her to look at him. "What's wrong?" he demanded.

"Nothing's wrong," she claimed, staring at the knot of his burgundy tie.

"Who are you trying to kid? You look like you just lost your best friend."

"I'm just tired, that's all."

She had the distinct feeling that if the door to the hall hadn't been open, he'd have kissed her. As it was, he released her chin and squeezed her shoulder. "If you want to take the rest of the day off—"

"No, I'm fine. Really." Going home wouldn't help.

"If you're sure."

"I'm sure."

When he smiled, she breathed a sigh of relief. A moment later she ushered the man from MGM in and went to work.

The rest of the day was an unmitigated disaster. At ten Jared needed a file while he was on the phone, and she broke two nails trying to find it. At eleven she tripped over a cable in engineering and dumped coffee down the front of her white skirt. After lunch she banged her knee on the corner of her desk drawer, giving herself a bruise and a run at the same time.

At 2:45 Jared left for his three o'clock meeting, and at 3:15 it started raining—hard and steady. Rachel went back to the weather department, tucked into a closet between the newsroom and the studio. The weatherman told her there was no letup in sight until late that night. The girls' game would be rained out.

And at five Rachel's world came crashing down around her shoulders.

Jared wasn't expected back until tomorrow, and Mike was late picking her up, probably, she assumed, due to the rain. She was in Jared's office searching through a stack of videocassettes, looking for an audition tape from a prospective news reporter so she could return it to the newsroom, when she came across a tape with a label from a St. Louis station, bearing her name. Not Rachel Fredrick. Not even Rachel Harding. Simply Rachel Anne.

Her throat closed and shut off her breath. She dropped the cassette as if it were a live wire. It crashed against the desk and fell to the floor. Suddenly light-headed, she closed her eyes and groped for the edge of the desk.

There was no need to play the tape. She knew what was on it. Oh, God, she knew!

"Rachel?"

At the sound of Jared's voice Rachel whirled to face him. Dizziness landed her in the chair behind his desk. Not able to look at him, she covered her face with shaking hands.

"Rachel, what's wrong?"

Eyes closed, she heard him come around the desk, heard his shoe connect with the cassette on the floor. A strained silence filled the room.

Rachel forced her hands to her lap and opened her eyes in time to see Jared bend down and pick up the tape. "How long have you known?" she whispered, her head spinning almost as fast as the room itself.

Jared straightened, the cassette dangling in his grasp. "I *don't* know. I haven't played the tape."

Two huge tears rolled down her cheeks. "You . . . haven't?"

"No."

She shook her head, bewildered. "Why?"

"Because I wanted you to trust me enough to tell me yourself. Because whatever it is you're hiding doesn't really matter. It has nothing to do with us. Don't you know," he said fiercely, "that *nothing* in your past can change the way I feel about you?"

Coldness seeped over her. She stood and gave Jared a choked laugh. "You won't say that after you watch that tape."

"I don't want to watch the damned tape." He flipped open the hinged door of the cassette with his thumb and started ripping the tape out. "I *won't* watch it."

Rachel stared, stunned, as yards and yards of ruined tape piled up at Jared's feet.

"Why?" She raised her gaze to his. "All my ugly little secrets are on that tape. Things you need to know about me."

"If they're important, you'll tell me yourself. If they're not, you won't. Like I said, whatever you're hiding can't change how I feel. I love you, Rachel."

"Excuse me. I'll come back later."

The cold in Rachel's bones turned to ice at the sound of the reporter's smooth voice behind her. Rage like she'd never felt in her life consumed her. Fair or not, here was someone she could blame. He'd come here and stuck his nose in her business, ruining any chance she might have had for happiness, for a normal life. She glared at Lyle Shotz, remembering the way he had hounded her in St. Louis.

Shotz grinned. "Guess I'm luckier than Sutton. By the look on your face, if you had a gun in your hand, I'd be dead."

Jared stiffened in shock.

At the look on his face Rachel cried out.

Jared took one look at Rachel's haunted eyes and pale face and knew he'd meant what he said. Whatever Shotz was hinting at, Jared didn't care. Something about a gun and maybe a dead man, and he didn't care. He only cared that Rachel not hurt anymore.

"She doesn't need a gun to deal with a weasel like you," Jared said between clenched teeth. "Apologize."

"The hell I will."

Blind with fury, Jared grabbed Shotz by the throat. He wanted to kill the bastard. "Apologize. *Now.*"

Shotz, his face turning purple, mumbled something unintelligible.

Jared heard nothing beyond the blood pounding in his ears. He shoved Shotz against the wall. "Repeat after me: Ms. Fredrick, I'm *very* sorry. Say it."

"C-Can't," Shotz managed.

"Say it!"

"She's . . . gone," Shotz said with a gasp.

When Jared loosened his hold to turn and look for Rachel, Shotz slid down the wall, gasping for breath. Jared ignored him. *She's gone.*

Out the front window he caught sight of the red Mustang pulling away from the curb, driving off in the rain.

She's gone.

With cold purpose Jared turned back to Shotz, who was just rising from the floor. "Get out of my sight and out of this station. You're fired."

Shotz straightened the collar of his plaid shirt and smirked. "You can't do that. I've got a contract."

"Not anymore, you don't."

Rachel could tell Mike knew something was wrong, but she was grateful he didn't ask questions. When they got home, she learned that Caro's game being rained out hadn't put a damper on the slumber party. With her daughter gone for the night and Mike still planning on going to Freddy's, Rachel went to her room and threw herself on the bed, shivering uncontrollably.

If they're important, you'll tell me yourself. If they're not, you won't.

By his words Jared was letting her off the hook. He said her past didn't matter, wouldn't change the way he felt. And he meant it. She couldn't imagine how much faith he must have had in her to ignore that tape. How much strength. How much love. He really believed her past wouldn't matter.

But only because he didn't realize that when her past came to light, as it would, it could destroy him. The vicious gossip would start again. It would affect his life, his daughter's life, his standing in the community.

She couldn't do that to him. She loved him too much to make him pay for her past. And she owed him, for the trust he placed in her hands, letting her make the decision whether or not to tell him the truth. She owed him.

She owed him more than just the truth. She owed him a peaceful life free of all the turmoil and pain she would bring him. But dear God, the thought of leaving him took her breath away. If she lay there and thought about life without him, she would never find the courage to do what she had to do.

With a deep breath and an angry swipe at her tears, she forced herself from the bed.

The walk up Jared's sidewalk at 10:20 that night was the longest she'd ever made in her life. By the time she reached for the doorbell, her hands were shaking so badly, she missed the button and had to aim again. She hit it on the third try.

She wiped her sweaty palms on her jeans.

It seemed as if she stood there forever. He was home. His car was in the driveway, and there were lights on in the house. Would he answer the door? Would she have the nerve to do what had to be done?

The heavy oak door swung inward, and there he stood. He was barefoot but still had his slacks on. His coat and tie were gone, shirt unbuttoned and hanging loose. Tiredness was etched across his face. And his expression was blank.

Rachel panicked. This was a mistake. She should have waited. They should have met in some neutral corner for her confession.

She stood on his doorstep, more uncertain than she'd ever been in her life. But there was one thing she was certain about. She took a deep breath and looked him right in the eye, ignoring the fact that her chin trembled and her vision was clouded with moisture. "I'm sorry I didn't trust you. I'm ready to tell you now."

The thread of tension holding him motionless snapped. He let out a harsh breath as his arms came around her and crushed her to his chest.

"Oh, Rachel, Rachel," he said. He buried his face in her hair. "I was afraid you wouldn't come."

Rachel felt his heart answer the thundering in her own chest. His arms were like steel, and she reveled in the fierceness of his embrace, knowing full well it might be the last time she ever experienced heaven.

Her heart quailed. How could she give him up?

Yet how could she not? For to stay with him, if he still wanted her after learning the truth, would be the worst thing she could do to him.

Her resolve firmed, she pulled free of his arms.

Jared took her by the hand and led her to the sofa in the den. He sat beside her and held on to her hand. "You don't have to tell me anything."

"Yes," she said, "I do. I should have told you the day we met."

"All right, then tell me what you think you have to, so we can put it behind us."

Rachel hung her head and stared at their joined hands. "This isn't exactly the kind of thing that can be ignored."

"Rachel, I love you."

She raised her gaze and saw the truth of his love in his eyes. Her vision blurred. "I love you, too, more than anything. I'm so ashamed for not telling you about my past before now. It's inexcusable, but I was afraid."

"Of what I'd think?"

"I guess."

Suddenly, touching him, holding his hand, was too much. She couldn't say what needed to be said while touching him. She sprang from the sofa and stood before the sliding glass doors, staring out at the pool. "Remember when I told you about my retiring from modeling?"

"When you wanted a calmer life. When you decided to become a secretary."

"Yes. But there were people who didn't believe such a simple explanation. There was this newspaper reporter in St. Louis. Carl Sutton." Just saying his name turned her hands to ice.

"The one Shotz mentioned?"

"Shotz and Sutton were friends. I'd known them both for years, but not well. While I was still modeling, Sutton made a couple of passes at me, but I brushed him off. When I retired, he thought I was lying about my reasons. He was used to dirt and scandal. He thought for sure I was hiding something."

Rachel rubbed her arms to warm them. "He started following me around, confronting me, generally making a nuisance of himself. Friends started teasing me about how often I was seen with him right behind me. He . . . became obsessed, I guess. With the story he wanted, and with me."

On the sofa Jared struggled with the urge to go to her and hold her. But she needed to do this her way, so he clenched his fists and sat still.

"Then, when school was out for the summer, Hank took the kids to visit his mother in Nashville. She'd been bugging us to visit for ages. I had to work that week, but I planned to join them for the weekend. The night before I was to leave, Sutton broke into the house."

Jared picked up his half-empty drink from the coffee table and downed it. He knew what was coming. God, he knew. Sutton was the man who attacked her. He wanted to stop her, to tell her she didn't have to do this.

"I was asleep. A noise woke me. I got scared. We'd had several burglaries in the neighborhood. Hank had bought a gun months earlier and insisted on keeping it in the nightstand. I . . . I got it out and—"

Her voice broke.

Jared couldn't stand it anymore. He crossed the room and took her in his arms. "It's all right," he told her.

She pushed him away, a wild look in her eyes. "It's *not* all right. I killed him! I shot a man dead in my own bedroom!"

Although shocked, Jared didn't for a minute believe that was all there was to her story. "He was the one, wasn't he? The one who attacked you."

She squeezed her eyes shut. When she reopened them, they were dull and blank. Her voice was lifeless. "I could hear someone coming down the hall toward the bedroom. The door opened, the light came on. I couldn't believe it when I recognized him."

She shook her head at the memory. "There I'd been, terrified of being murdered in my bed, and it was only Carl, making a pest out of himself again. I got so angry, I jumped out of bed and started screaming at him to get out."

When it seemed she wouldn't go on, Jared prodded. "But he didn't."

"No," she whispered. "He didn't. He grabbed me and forced me down on the bed, yelling at me that he was tired of being teased, tired of me not giving him the story he wanted. He said . . . said he'd get a story one way or the other."

She swiped at her lips with her tongue and stared somewhere in the middle of Jared's chest.

"I didn't even remember I had the gun in my hand. I tried to get away from him, but he held me down. When I realized he was going to . . . to rape me, I . . . I panicked. We fought. The first I realized I still had the gun was when it went off."

Jared pulled her back into his arms and held her tight. She shook violently against him. "I'm sorry. I'm so sorry you had to go through that. No man has the right to do what he tried. I'm glad he's dead," he said fiercely. "Do you hear me? I'm glad he's dead. If he wasn't, I'd want to kill him myself."

She pulled back and looked at him. Her eyes weren't blank any longer; they were haunted again. "It was an accident."

"Of course it was, I know that."

She gave a harsh laugh and turned away. "You're one of the few, then."

"What do you mean?" he asked carefully. "Who could possibly say it wasn't an accident?"

"Oh, the district attorney, for one."

Jared felt a chill race down his spine. "What?"

"And exactly half of the jury."

"You went to trial?" he asked, outraged. "For what? For defending yourself?"

"First-degree murder."

"*What?*"

"The prosecution said I was having an affair with him. That when he threatened to print it in the paper, I killed him."

"And people *believed* that?"

"Did they ever. The press ate it up. There's nothing like one of their own being killed to get the press to pull together. Shotz was the worst of them. He wouldn't quit."

Jared strove to keep his voice calm. "You were obviously acquitted."

She turned a blank smile on him. "Guess again."

"What are you saying? If you'd been convicted, you wouldn't be here now."

"Ever hear of a hung jury?"

Jared could only stare at her in shock.

"The jury couldn't reach a verdict. I guess I was just lucky the D.A. didn't ask for a new trial."

Jared felt sick. Good God, to have something like that hanging over her head. It wasn't fair, dammit. It wasn't right. "Surely, you testified. Surely, you told them the truth. How could they not have believed you?"

She gave him another harsh laugh. "How can I blame the jury, when my own husband didn't believe me?"

Jared let out a word he didn't normally use in mixed company.

Rachel ignored him. "Not that Hank believed I was having an affair with Sutton. On the contrary, he said he knew better. He also said he knew Sutton would never have tried to rape me, because Hank had already told him I was lousy in bed."

So that's where her insecurity had come from that night they'd made love. "I told you before, the man was a fool. Or a liar. If he didn't believe any of that, how did he explain Sutton being in your bedroom?"

She closed her eyes and tilted her head back. "He said I lured him with the promise of a story, then shot him in anger when he wouldn't sleep with me."

Jared swore. When she turned away, he stopped her with a hand to her chin. "What happened to you was terrible. I ache for how much it must have hurt. But, dammit, Rachel, how could you possibly think any of that would affect how I feel about you?"

"I guess because I'm the biggest fool of all."

"Come here." He held out his arms.

"There's more, Jared."

"I don't care."

She moved away from him. "Well, I do. Because this part will affect you."

"Try me."

Rachel was tired. So damned tired. But she was almost through. She'd told him almost everything. Just a little more, then she could rest.

"After the trial, the press, Shotz in particular, wouldn't let it die. I was notorious. The talk of the town. 'Did she or didn't she?' My situation at work became impossible, so I quit and found another job. And another. Every time it got around just who I was, the talk would start all over again."

"So you came here and disguised yourself, hoping no one would recognize you."

"Yes."

"You've been without your disguise for weeks, and no one's said anything, have they?"

"No, but they will. It's only a matter of time. If I don't give Shotz an interview, it'll be all over town."

"I fired him."

She turned and stared out at the swimming pool. "It'll be all over town that much faster then."

When she remained silent, Jared said, "Is that it?"

"Is that it?" she cried, whirling toward him. "Isn't that enough? Isn't it enough that I'll be ostracized again? That my kids will be exposed to all the talk, all the speculation?"

"If we stand together—"

"Together?" she cried. "We can't be together, don't you see? You're an important man in this city. You have to think of your reputation. You have to think of Debbie, and what the talk will do to her. We can't be together. We *can't.*"

"You don't mean that."

"Of course I mean it. How do you think people are going to react when they find out your secretary was tried for murder? That she was never even acquitted? If you don't think I'm guilty, that makes seven of you. You, and six jurors."

"And the D.A.," Jared retorted. "He could have had you tried again because of that hung jury. If he hadn't believed you, he would have done it in a minute."

"He didn't believe me. He just didn't want to waste the taxpayers' money with a new trial that could end in another hung jury. Everyone else—"

"To hell with everyone else! I love you!"

A sharp sob escaped before Rachel could hold it back. "And how long will that last?" she cried. "How long can you take the gossip and rumors before you start hating me?" She turned and fled for the door.

"What are you going to do, run away again?"

His words stopped her. She swiped at her damp cheeks before turning to face him. "If that's what it takes to keep my sanity, to keep my children from having to deal with taunts about their murdering mother, if that's what it takes to keep you from being tarred with the same brush, then yes, I'll run."

"It won't work, Rachel," he said, his gaze holding her in place. "No matter where you run, you'll never forget. Not your past, not me." He stalked her across the room. "You love me, and I love you. You know we belong together."

Rachel wanted nothing more at that moment than to hurl herself into his arms. But she couldn't. She had to get away, had to think, plan, decide what to do next. Yes, she loved him. She loved him so much, it was killing her. But there could be nothing between them now. A man in Jared's position couldn't afford the type of publicity she would bring him. She should have known that from the beginning.

She *had* known it. She had simply ignored it. The time for ignoring was past. "Accept it, Jared. I have to leave, for both our sakes."

"I don't accept it. And I damn sure don't appreciate you making my decisions for me. I love you. I want you in my life. And I'm willing to bet our kids are a hell of a lot stronger than you're giving them credit for. If you leave, you leave because you don't love me, not because you think you're doing what's best for me. What's best for me is you."

She stood frozen in the doorway, shaking, trying to swallow.

"Look me in the eye and tell me you don't love me," he demanded.

Rachel didn't even think of trying. She knew the lie would not come out. "You know I can't."

"Then stay," he said firmly. "Stay with me, love me, let me love you. If there's talk—"

"If?" she cried. "Of course there'll be talk. Shotz will never let it go."

"Then we'll fight him. Together. You and me. Just . . . *stay*."

Oh, God, oh, God, how could she? Yet how could she not?

He stepped closer, so close she could see the pain in his eyes. "Stay," he said again.

She gripped the doorframe until her fingers went numb. She bit her lip and tried to clear her vision.

He held out his hand toward her. "Stay. If you want me to beg, I'll beg. Just stay. Please."

Please? This big, strong man loved her enough to beg? "Jared," she whispered. She was in his arms in less than a second. "Oh, Jared, I love you, I love you."

His arms trembled as he held her and covered her face with frantic kisses. "I love you, too, so damn much. Swear you'll never scare me like that again. I couldn't stand it if you left me."

"Are you sure?" She held his face in her hands and searched his eyes. "Are you sure you want to—"

"I've never been more sure of anything in my life. You're not leaving me. Say it. Say it."

On a broken sob she said it. "I won't leave you."

"Swear it," he demanded.

"I swear it."

Then, with a harsh groan, he kissed her. He had to, or die. At the thought of how close he'd come to losing her, he shuddered. He filled himself with her taste, her soft scent. He filled his head with her response, his arms with her body, his hand with her breast. Want and need clawed at him.

"You almost left me," he accused between kisses.

"I would have died without you." She kissed his jaw, his neck.

He pulled her shirttail from her jeans and ran his hands up her back. "I want you. Here. Now."

"Yes." She tugged his unbuttoned shirt down his arms. "Here. Now."

Mindlessly, frantically, he took her down on the carpet amid their discarded clothes. No tender kisses, no soft words. No holding back. Just Rachel, taking him into her body and giving him back his soul. Her fingers dug into his backside, urging him on, faster, harder. The heat of her, the cries she made in the back of her throat, seared his brain.

Their loving was raw and hot and glorious, and he couldn't hold back. He plunged into her again and again until his name burst from her lips, and hers from his, in a mutual release more powerful than anything he'd ever felt.

When Jared could breathe again, when he thought his quivering muscles were his to command once more, he lifted Rachel in his arms and carried her upstairs to his bed. They lay there, sweat-slicked bodies entwined, hearts still thundering.

Rachel turned to kiss his shoulder. Something on the bedside table caught her eye, and she smiled. "You kept them," she said in wonder.

Jared followed her gaze and spotted the tacky green glasses she'd worn so long ago. They'd been on his nightstand since he'd taken them from her in Las Vegas.

"Why?" she asked, puzzled. "I thought you hated them."

Jared nuzzled his face against the golden hair spread out in disarray across his pillow. "Sometimes, I felt like they were the only part of you I could hold on to."

Rachel wrapped her arms around him and squeezed. "You can hold on to all or any part of me as long as you want, Jared Morgan."

He raised his head slowly and cupped her face in his hands. "Would you be willing to put that in writing, Rachel Fredrick?"

"In writing?"

"With witnesses?"

"What witnesses?"

"Any witnesses you want, as long as one of them's a minister, or at least a justice of the peace."

Her eyes widened. She simply stared at him and tried to swallow, but the lump in her throat was too big.

"I love you, Rachel. I'm asking you to marry me."

She blinked, and tears ran down her temples. "Oh, Jared," she breathed. "Oh, yes! Yes! Yes! Yes!" She planted kisses all over his face, laughing and crying at the same time.

THE EDITOR'S CORNER

Come join the celebration next month when LOVE-SWEPT reaches its tenth anniversary! When the line was started, we made a very important change in the way romance was being published. At the time, most romance authors published under a pseudonym, but we were so proud of our authors that we wanted to give them the credit and personal recognition they deserved. Since then LOVESWEPT authors have always written under their own names and their pictures appear on the inside covers of the books.

Right from the beginning LOVESWEPT was at the cutting edge, and as our readership changes, we change with them. In the process, we have nurtured writing stars, not only for romance, but for the publishing industry as a whole. We're proud of LOVESWEPT and the authors whose words we have brought to countless readers over the last ten years.

The lineup next month is indeed something to be proud about, with romances from five authors who have been steady—and stellar—contributors to LOVESWEPT since the very beginning and one up-and-coming name. Further, each of these six books carries a special anniversary message from the author to you. So don't let the good times pass you by. Pick up all six books, then sit back and enjoy!

The first of these treasures is **WILDFIRE**, LOVE-SWEPT #618 by Billie Green. Nobody can set aflame a woman's passion like Tanner West. He's spent his life breaking the rules—and more than a few hearts—and makes being bad seem awfully good. Though small-town Texas lawyer Rae Anderson wants a man who'd care for her and give her children, she finds herself rising to Tanner's challenge to walk on the wild side. This breathtaking romance is just what you've come to expect from super-talented Billie!

Kay Hooper continues her *Men of Mysteries Past* series with **THE TROUBLE WITH JARED**, LOVESWEPT #619. Years before, Jared Chavalier had been obsessed by Danica Gray, but her career as a gemologist had driven them apart. Now she arrives in San Francisco to work on the Mysteries Past exhibit of jewelry and discovers Jared there. And with a dangerous thief afoot, Jared must risk all to protect the only woman he's ever loved. Kay pulls out all the stops with this utterly stunning love story.

WHAT EMILY WANTS, LOVESWEPT #620 by Fayrene Preston, shocks even Emily Stanton herself, but she accepts Jay Barrett's bargain—ten days of her company for the money she so desperately needs. The arrangement is supposed to be platonic, but Emily soon finds she'll do just about anything . . . except let herself fall in love with the man whose probing questions drive her into hiding the truth. Fayrene delivers an intensely emotional and riveting read with this different kind of romance.

'TIL WE MEET AGAIN, LOVESWEPT #621 by Helen Mittermeyer, brings Cole Whitford and Fidelia Peters together at a high school reunion years after she'd disappeared from his life. She's never told him the heartbreaking reason she'd left town, and once the silken web of memories ensnares them both, they have to decide whether to let the past divide them once more . . . or to admit to a love that time has made only more precious. Shimmering with heartfelt emotion, **'TIL WE MEET AGAIN** is Helen at her finest.

Romantic adventure has never been as spellbinding as **STAR-SPANGLED BRIDE**, LOVESWEPT #622 by Iris Johansen. When news station mogul Gabe Falkner is taken by terrorists, he doesn't expect anyone to come to his rescue, least of all a golden-haired angel. But photojournalist Ronnie Dalton would dare anything to set free the man who'd saved her from death years ago, the one man she's always adored, the only man she dares not love. Iris works her bestselling magic with this highly sensual romance.

Last is **THE DOCTOR TAKES A WIFE**, LOVESWEPT #623 by Kimberli Wagner. The doctor is Connor MacLeod, a giant of a Scot who pours all his emotions into his work, but whose heart doesn't come alive until he meets jockey Alix Benton. For the first time since the night her life was nearly ruined, Alix doesn't fear a man's touch. Then suspicious accidents begin to happen, and Connor must face the greatest danger to become Alix's hero. Kimberli brings her special touch of humor and sizzling desire to this terrific romance.

On sale this month from Bantam are four spectacular women's fiction novels. From *New York Times* bestselling author Amanda Quick comes **DANGEROUS**, a breathtaking tale of an impetuous miss—and a passion that leads to peril. Boldness draws Prudence Merryweather into one dangerous episode after another, while the notorious Earl of Angelstone finds himself torn between a raging hunger to possess her and a driving need to keep her safe.

Patricia Potter's new novel, **RENEGADE**, proves that she is a master storyteller of historical romance. Set during the tumultuous days right after the Civil War, **RENEGADE** is the passionate tale of Rhys Redding, the Welsh adventurer who first appeared in **LIGHTNING** and Susannah Fallon, who must trust Rhys with her life while on a journey through the lawless South.

Pamela Simpson follows the success of **FORTUNE'S CHILD** with the contemporary novel **MIRROR, MIRROR**. When an unexpected inheritance entangles Alexandra Wyatt with a powerful family, Allie finds herself falling in love. And as she succumbs to Rafe Sloan's seductive power, she comes to suspect that he knows something of the murder she'd witnessed as a child.

In a dazzling debut, Geralyn Dawson delivers **THE TEXAN'S BRIDE**, the second book in Bantam's series of ONCE UPON A TIME romances. Katie Starr knows the rugged Texan is trouble the moment he steps into her father's inn, yet even as Branch is teasing his way into the lonely young widow's heart, Katie fears her secret would surely drive him away from her.

Also on sale this month in the Doubleday hardcover edition is **MOONLIGHT, MADNESS, AND MAGIC**, an anthology of original novellas by Suzanne Forster, Charlotte Hughes, and Olivia Rupprecht, in which a journal and a golden locket hold the secret to breaking an ancient family curse.

Happy reading!

With warmest wishes,

Nita Taublib

Nita Taublib
Associate Publisher

OFFICIAL RULES TO WINNERS CLASSIC SWEEPSTAKES

No Purchase necessary. To enter the sweepstakes follow instructions found elsewhere in this offer. You can also enter the sweepstakes by hand printing your name, address, city, state and zip code on a 3" x 5" piece of paper and mailing it to: Winners Classic Sweepstakes, P.O. Box 785, Gibbstown, NJ 08027. Mail each entry separately. Sweepstakes begins 12/1/91. Entries must be received by 6/1/93. Some presentations of this sweepstakes may feature a deadline for the Early Bird prize. If the offer you receive does, then to be eligible for the Early Bird prize your entry must be received according to the Early Bird date specified. Not responsible for lost, late, damaged, misdirected, illegible or postage due mail. Mechanically reproduced entries are not eligible. All entries become property of the sponsor and will not be returned.

Prize Selection/Validations: Winners will be selected in random drawings on or about 7/30/93, by VENTURA ASSOCIATES, INC., an independent judging organization whose decisions are final. Odds of winning are determined by total number of entries received. Circulation of this sweepstakes is estimated not to exceed 200 million. Entrants need not be present to win. All prizes are guaranteed to be awarded and delivered to winners. Winners will be notified by mail and may be required to complete an affidavit of eligibility and release of liability which must be returned within 14 days of date of notification or alternate winners will be selected. Any guest of a trip winner will also be required to execute a release of liability. Any prize notification letter or any prize returned to a participating sponsor, Bantam Doubleday Dell Publishing Group, Inc., its participating divisions or subsidiaries, or VENTURA ASSOCIATES, INC. as undeliverable will be awarded to an alternate winner. Prizes are not transferable. No multiple prize winners except as may be necessary due to unavailability, in which case a prize of equal or greater value will be awarded. Prizes will be awarded approximately 90 days after the drawing. All taxes, automobile license and registration fees, if applicable, are the sole responsibility of the winners. Entry constitutes permission (except where prohibited) to use winners' names and likenesses for publicity purposes without further or other compensation.

Participation: This sweepstakes is open to residents of the United States and Canada, except for the province of Quebec. This sweepstakes is sponsored by Bantam Doubleday Dell Publishing Group, Inc. (BDD), 666 Fifth Avenue, New York, NY 10103. Versions of this sweepstakes with different graphics will be offered in conjunction with various solicitations or promotions by different subsidiaries and divisions of BDD. Employees and their families of BDD, its division, subsidiaries, advertising agencies, and VENTURA ASSOCIATES, INC., are not eligible.

Canadian residents, in order to win, must first correctly answer a time limited arithmetical skill testing question. Void in Quebec and wherever prohibited or restricted by law. Subject to all federal, state, local and provincial laws and regulations.

Prizes: The following values for prizes are determined by the manufacturers' suggested retail prices or by what these items are currently known to be selling for at the time this offer was published. Approximate retail values include handling and delivery of prizes. Estimated maximum retail value of prizes: 1 Grand Prize ($27,500 if merchandise or $25,000 Cash); 1 First Prize ($3,000); 5 Second Prizes ($400 each); 35 Third Prizes ($100 each); 1,000 Fourth Prizes ($9.00 each) ; 1 Early Bird Prize ($5,000); Total approximate maximum retail value is $50,000. Winners will have the option of selecting any prize offered at level won. Automobile winner must have a valid driver's license at the time the car is awarded. Trips are subject to space and departure availability. Certain black-out dates may apply. Travel must be completed within one year from the time the prize is awarded. Minors must be accompanied by an adult. Prizes won by minors will be awarded in the name of parent or legal guardian.

For a list of Major Prize Winners (available after 7/30/93): send a self-addressed, stamped envelope entirely separate from your entry to: Winners Classic Sweepstakes Winners, P.O. Box 825, Gibbstown, NJ 08027. Requests must be received by 6/1/93. DO NOT SEND ANY OTHER CORRESPONDENCE TO THIS P.O. BOX.

SWP 9/92